REWIND AND PLAY

Hostel diaries of a frustrated B. Tech

TreeShade Books

www.treeshadebooks.com

REWIND AND PLAY

Hostel diaries of a frustrated B. Tech

TreeShade Books

REWIND & PLAY

Hostel diaries of a frustrated B. Tech

ISBN : 9788193642474

Published by
TreeShade Books (VB Performance LLP)
Ansal Corporate Park, Sector142, Noida, Uttar Pradesh - 201305, India
Email - publish@TreeShadeBooks.com
www.TreeShadeBooks.com

Printed and Bound in India by
Gopsons Papers Ltd., A-2 Sector 64, Noida - 201301, India

Cover Design: Munisha Nanda
Cover Caricature: Tarun Gautam

To our daughter
Radhika

Only when the happiness is past and we look back on, it do we suddenly realize—sometimes with astonishment—how happy we had been.
—Nikos Kazantzakis, Zorba the Greek

ACKNOWLEDGEMENTS

When I embarked on my mission to write this book, I was confident that I would be alone. Alone with my thoughts and my imagination. But today when I look back, I realize nothing could have been further from the truth. Though we think we walk alone, our journeys are seldom by ourselves. Knowingly or unknowingly; directly or indirectly there are several others who accompany us and spur us along.

I would like to thank those who've made my journey worthwhile.

There are several authors who have written about their college days and I would like to thank them for being the stimuli for the book. In fact, this book was written with the intent to prove that my college days were much more fun-filled than theirs! Of course, this assertion can only be evaluated by the readers who I hope shall reach out to me with their feedback.

I would like to thank my alma maters IIM Lucknow and Kurukshetra University. The IIM Lucknow alumni and faculty for inspiring me to dream and push the boundaries. The historic city of Kurukshetra—the battleground of the epic *Mahabharata*—for the memories, friends and learnings for a lifetime.

I've been fortunate to have around me authors, or more appropriately fellow patients, infected by the writer's bug—Dr Nitish Dogra, Vineet Bajpai, Neeraj Verma and Suraj Goswami—

who have provided valuable inputs during the process.

My mother, for being a pillar of strength and for instilling the right values in me.

Whatever creative genes I have, I owe them to my father. I have him to thank for initiating me into the world of books.

Pragya, my wife, for patiently listening to my ideas—however ludicrous they may have been!

I owe a lot to the organizations I worked at, for the opportunities and the exposure. Thanks to them, I have travelled a considerable part of the world and experienced different cultures.

To the TreeShade Books team for their professional approach during the entire publication process. Thank you, Vineet Bajpai, for being an inspiration and for guiding me along in the publication process.

My editor, Pritsikha Anil, for her stellar editing work, I have utmost gratefulness.

To Vivek Merani, for spearheading the digital push behind marketing the book.

My daughter, Radhika, for lighting up our lives. Someday when she is growing up, trying to understand life, I hope she will pick up this book and find some nuggets from her father's early years.

Bless you.

THE GLOVE

'Ladies and gentlemen, a very good evening once again. Your wait is finally over. It's now time for the highlight of the evening—the Pathbreaker's Shining Beacon awards ceremony. At PathBreakers, we aim to bring together the best of technology and honour their contributors,' announced the emcee of the evening in her well-modulated voice.

'To announce the awards in this segment, I'd like to call on stage, Roberto. For those of you who don't know Roberto, he is the most handsome, articulate, well-read, multilingual person you would have ever met.'

Onto the stage walked a man with the physique of Sean Connery and the handsome face of Brad Pitt. The only aspect that gave away the fact was that it was a humanoid, and not a human being, was the walk. The walk, though fairly smooth and almost human-like, had a faint resemblance to Michael Jackson's moonwalk.

'Hi Elena,' said Roberto in a heavy baritone and stretched out his hand in a smooth, controlled motion.

'Hi Roberto,' replied a smiling Elena.

The audience roared and clapped wildly.

Roberto raised his hand and acknowledged the audience.

Over the years, the awards ceremony organized by the Pathbreaker's Corporation had become a sought-after annual event for leading technology companies, customers and consultants. Every year, the corporation unveiled one of its own products, and also honoured other companies that stretched the boundaries of product innovation. This year their in-house product innovation was Roberto, the humanoid that was developed to deliver superior customer service for several industries.

The people who followed the awards very closely belonged to the world's leading consumer technology companies. Raghav Diwan, who was sitting in the second row of the auditorium at Hilton Times Square, was one of them.

'And to announce the winner of the most innovative consumer product of the year, I would like to call on stage the Founder and CEO of the Pathbreakers Group, Mr Andrew Hartmann,' said Roberto with the ease of a seasoned emcee.

Raghav watched in awe as one of his idols from the business fraternity made his way onto the large stage. For Raghav, it was a dream come true to be in the same room as Hartmann.

'And the nominees for the award are 4D Home Theatre from Alpha Technologies, Wearable Smart phone from VisionTek and Ultra Chef from Utronics,' said Roberto.

Raghav could suddenly feel his heart pound harder. What would he say on stage if he won the award? What explanation could he give to the senior management if he lost? Just then, his phone vibrated and he saw a WhatsApp message from his wife Tarana.

'Has your award been announced?'

He quickly typed, 'About to be. Fingers crossed.'

'Oh my god! All the best. Luv you.'

Hartmann took the microphone and the envelope with the winner's name from Roberto and said, 'I'm pleased to see new companies that have made it to the list and am also impressed with the themes they have covered. Without further ado, I'm going to announce the winner of the award for the most innovative consumer product of the year.'

'It is the Glove from VisionTek,' said Hartmann excitedly.

'I invite Mr Raghav Diwan, Division Head—Consumer Products, VisionTek, to collect the award,' said Roberto, clapping his robotic hands loudly.

Raghav got up from his seat, buttoned his jacket and walked confidently towards the stage to receive the award from Hartmann. As he got onto the stage, he could see the video of the Glove, with the catchphrase 'smartphones are a part of your life, now they're a part of your body' playing on the gigantic screen.

The visual showed a model with her hand next to her ear and moving her lips. Slowly, she revealed a sleek device strapped on her palm. With the song from Carly Rae Jepsen 'Call me maybe' playing in the background, the effect was simply phenomenal.

Since its launch three months ago, the Glove had shown steady sales and winning the award was an endorsement of its growing popularity. The fifteen-second walk to the stage was worth the endless nights that Raghav and his team had put in through the last three years.

The Glove looked rugged and sexy. It was like the finger cut-out gloves that bikers wore. But behind the rugged looks was state-of-the-art wearable technology. The top of the Glove had a flexible touchscreen with conductive polymer compounds. Circuits in the palm were connected to neoprene buttons that allowed the fingers of the palm to press the button and activate the phone. The Glove was powered by stretchy supercapacitors using ribbons of graphene. The circuitry was completely insulated by a water-resistant material. All these features made it far superior to any smartphone in the market. The upwardly mobile youth had already given the Glove their thumbs up and were driving the majority of the sales.

At the awards dinner, Raghav was the cynosure of all eyes. Industry veterans, the press and even some of the competitors were jostling to get a piece of him. Raghav savoured every moment of the attention.

Raghav suddenly realized that in all the excitement, he'd forgotten to tell his wife that he'd won. He quickly sent her a message on WhatsApp, 'Time to open up the bubbly ☺'

Driving back home to New Jersey from the Hilton, Raghav's mind was filled with thoughts of the future. First was the vice-president position that he had set his eyes upon. Second was the fact that he would be able to comfortably pay for the new house he and his wife had bought in the Princeton suburb of New Jersey. Third may have been a little far-fetched but it was something he strongly desired. It was buying a small sailboat that had recently caught his fancy. He really liked the name 'Peppermint' that his younger son Vishal had suggested.

Raghav and Tarana had been living in the USA for over fourteen years. They had met while working for the same company in Mumbai, India. After a year of working, Raghav went on to pursue his master's in electronics from an American university but they continued to keep in touch. Over time, their feelings for each other grew stronger and they decided to tie the knot.

Raghav received the Summa Cum Laude for graduating with distinction. He was intelligent, but so were the others in his class. What set him apart from his peers was his hunger—an insatiable hunger that possessed him to pursue his goals relentlessly.

Tarana focused on her career in the initial years of their marriage, but she later chose to stay at home to take care of their boys—Angad and Vishal—who were under the age of five. Raghav and Tarana loved the American way of life and considered themselves fortunate to be staying in the US. Both were now green card holders and wanted to give their kids the kind of childhood they could only dream of in India.

***

Raghav was sitting at his desk surfing through the pictures of the awards night on Financial Times, when the meeting reminder 'Project Delorian—Review' popped up on his screen. Rob Stiller, the COO of VisionTek, held this weekly progress meeting to take stock of their product line. The meeting brought together all the teams—product management, sales, quality, production, marketing and customer relations—on one platform.

'Great job Raghav on the award,' said Max Wolffe, Head of Marketing and Corporate Communication, giving Raghav a loud high-five.

'Wow, Raghav! I saw the pictures on Financial Times. They were terrific,' said Jane, congratulating him.

Rob walked in and took his usual place at the head of the table.

'Team, terrific win yesterday. Congratulations! I'm seeing reports of sales and customer requests and they all look very impressive. Inquiries since yesterday have seen a 250 per cent jump. So, guys, keep up the good work. But remember, it will be six months of very good sales before we are able to break even. Since production is going to go up substantially, we need to be extra cautious about the product quality. Raghav, we need to keep continuing with our tests.'

Raghav nodded his head and immediately typed out a message to his team asking them to prepare a rigorous test schedule for the next three months. The subject of the email was 'Let's not lose focus'.

***

'Tough day?' asked Tarana as she opened the door for Raghav.

'Yes, had back-to-back meetings.'

'Are the boys asleep?'

'Yes, they slept early today. Let me fix your dinner.'

Raghav ate his dinner, while Tarana sat with him.

'Today I had a chat with papa. He was finally able to use Skype,' said Tarana with a laugh.

'Great. It'll be nice for him to chat with the boys.'

'He was saying that the Archaeological Survey of India wants him to do a project as a consultant in Bhimbetka, Madhya Pradesh. He's interested, but not sure if he wants to get into all the travelling. He said wanted to discuss an idea with you. Call him when you have time.'

Raghav listened to her but didn't respond. He finished his dinner and took out his laptop and started working.

***

A few weeks later, Raghav received a phone call. It was Jane from the quality team.

'Howdy Raghav, I want to have a quick discussion with you. Can we meet for coffee?'

'Yeah, sure. Give me five minutes, please. Let me send Rob a report first.'

Jane was already there when Raghav reached the office café. Raghav ordered his usual hazelnut cappuccino and walked up to Jane's table.

Jane looked a bit anxious and got straight to the point.

'Raghav, I've been running some stress tests on the device. I've noticed after a certain number of usage hours; the battery starts to spark abruptly. It's very strange. I think we need to bring this to Rob's attention immediately.'

'Hmm. This is absurd. Our stress tests covered twice the number of standard operating hours. So, I don't understand what could be wrong,' said Raghav, concealing his worst fears.

'It's probably something on the design side of the Glove. The circuits are probably consuming more power and the supercapacitors are heating up. I don't know, Raghav. This is serious. I'm getting worried.'

'Why don't you run tests on some more samples? Meanwhile, I'll see what I can pick up on my side.'

Back at his desk, Raghav tried to analyze the situation. If this turned out to be a serious problem, then recalls were imminent. Sales were growing rapidly and were about to reach a quarter of a million. The negative press from this news would be catastrophic for the product. Raghav tried to wrap his mind around what was happening. He immediately called for an emergency team meeting.

After a couple of hours, Raghav called Jane. 'The team is analyzing the situation. I've given them a few days to come back with their findings. I'm travelling this week, but I will closely monitor the situation.'

'Okay, Raghav. Let me know if we should let Rob know,' said Jane.

'Let's wait for the findings.'

When Raghav got back home late in the evening, Tarana was returning with the kids from a play date. He tried to conceal his anxiety but Tarana could sense something was troubling him.

A few days later, Raghav was at JKF's duty-free bookstore after his return from a meeting with suppliers in Japan and France. He was flipping through the pages of the book 'Sailing: A Beginner's Handbook' when his vibrating phone distracted him. It was Jane.

'Hi Raghav. Got a call from Max this morning. There's been an accident with a Glove user. The battery sparked and the user's palm was burnt. He has been rushed to the hospital. Daily News picked up this news first and called Max for a press statement.'

'Oh shit! This serious,' said Raghav. 'Let me call Rob immediately.'

Raghav called Rob, and as expected Rob asked everyone to reach office for a debrief.

Raghav picked up his bags and rushed out of the airport. Though Raghav did not notice, this incident was all over the airport screens. The channels were having a field day playing the news in a loop. 'Breaking news: Young boy critical after smartphone catches fire in his palm,' screamed the headlines.

Raghav took a cab to the office in the city. He called his team to check on their findings. The bad news was that there was nothing conclusive yet on the root cause of the fire. Once in office, he dashed towards the elevator and then ran straight to the CEO Greg Duvall's conference room on the twenty-third floor. Just before he entered the room, he WhatsApped his wife, 'In office, something serious.'

Raghav had been to the executive floor several times in the past, but today was very different. The walls of the executive floor had beautiful wildlife photographs taken by Greg from his several visits to game reserves such as Kruger National park, Masai Mara and Serengeti. On an ordinary day they made for an interesting conversation, but today they were an avoidable distraction.

It was 7.30 a.m. when Rob and the others entered the conference room. Rob walked in and announced that Greg was travelling and would be joining over a call.

Rob quickly dialled Greg. Greg got on the line with a deep 'Hello.'

'Morning Greg, it's Rob. I have the entire team with me. After I spoke to you, I called the Daily News and told them that we'll issue a press statement only after our meeting.'

Greg spoke in his usual calm voice, 'Team, it's very unfortunate that this has happened. As much as we did not want this, the reality is we now have to deal with it. We'll need to quickly come up with an action plan. So, let's go around the table to take suggestions on how we can tackle this.'

The meeting didn't last long. Greg ended the call, asking everyone but Rob to leave.

Everyone huddled outside the conference room sharing their anxiety. Most people were stuck to their phones, checking the Internet and social media platforms.

Raghav was also checking his phone when Rob called him aside.

'Raghav.'

'Yeah, Rob.'

'Greg's message is that you'll need to leave VisionTek.'

He paused for a couple of seconds and added, 'With immediate effect.'

There was a short pause. Greg waited for Raghav to respond. When that didn't happen, he continued, 'I hope you understand. In the current situation, managing the media is very important and we have to show that we are taking tough steps. You'll get a severance package but avoid talking to the media or else there may be legal trouble.'

Raghav had nothing to say. He simply nodded his head, turned around and pressed the button for the elevator.

Though he'd been in corporate America for over a decade and had seen several lay-offs of colleagues and friends, this was the first time he was facing the situation. He felt as though he was leaving a dentist's chair after an extraction that caused no pain during the process but had left a dull throbbing pain thereafter.

The elevator door opened and a few executives got out and smiled at him. Raghav smiled back faintly, as if on autopilot. As the door closed, his eyes were drawn to a photograph on the wall opposite the elevator.

It was a picture of a lion sitting low in the Savannah, stalking an unsuspecting wildebeest.

INVITATION

Raghav quietly collected his supplies in a carton and walked out of his cabin. He moved across the floor and saw a few puzzled faces and a few sympathetic ones. Some of them wore a veneer of sympathy, but they were probably happy to see him go. Raghav took a cab home. His mobile phone was lying on the seat next to him but he didn't have the guts to pick it up to read the news. He already knew what the headlines would be. Division head of VisionTek fired.

'I was following the news. Raghav, this is really bad,' said Tarana.

'Yes. Only worse. They've asked me to leave.'

What? This is unbelievable!'

'It was expected. Don't think they had a choice,' said Raghav, smiling wryly.

Appearing to be in control, he went through all the details with Tarana.

Later that night, as they were about to sleep, Tarana held Raghav's hand.

'Don't worry. Things will work out,' she said, in a reassuring voice.

'Yeah. Let's see.'

Over the next few days, Raghav made a few more trips to the

office to complete the exit formalities. On one of his trips he met his friend Will Stanton, from the design team. Raghav and Will had worked together on several projects and shared a good rapport.

'Raghav, I met Peter Semenov from legal yesterday. There's talk the boy may sue VisionTek for a couple of million dollars. VisionTek may use the media to malign you and get the attention away from them,' said Will, looking very concerned.

'There was a whole team behind this project, not just me. So, why go after me?' said Raghav, swallowing hard and rubbing his chin nervously.

'You were the poster boy of the project. Going after you makes good media news and shifts the blame from the rest. As a matter of fact, it's quite simple,' said Will.

Raghav simply stared blankly at Will. He knew the cost of a legal battle was steep and with no job in hand he knew a catastrophe loomed ahead of him. He wondered if he should put his Lexus and Land Cruiser for sale in the used car market

***

One Sunday, Raghav was scanning his mailbox for job offers when the phone rang. It was Harpreet. Raghav and Harpreet were friends since their graduation days. Harpreet too lived in New Jersey. Though they had come to the US around the same time, their work lives had kept them so busy that they hardly met.

Raghav was fairly certain Harpreet would have read the news about the Glove debacle. So, he wondered if he should take the call. He was about to take the call, but then stopped himself.

'Raghav, your phone's ringing,' said Tarana.

'Yeah I know.'

'Aren't you going to answer it?'

'No.'

'Who is it?'

'Harpreet.'

***

Another month passed, but Raghav still had no job offers. Raghav always believed that his skills would be in great demand; so, when there were no job offers, it began to affect his self-esteem. Every single day that he was at home was like being in a prison alone with the burden of his failure. Every time he tried to pull himself out of this state, a household bill would appear from nowhere and push him back into the abyss of despair.

Tarana was worried about Raghav's behaviour. He seemed to be turning into a recluse. He was also very cold towards Tarana and the boys.

Another month passed and the situation was still the same.

Raghav got back home one evening after meeting an old colleague.

'How was the meeting?' asked Tarana.

'Well, he says he'll do something. So, let's see. He says the problem is that the entire incident was in the news. It is stuck in people's memory and that will take some time to fade.'

'Why don't you try shifting to another industry? You don't have to work in electronics design all your life. Why don't you try something else even if the money is a little less?'

'No, I won't do that,' Raghav retorted angrily. 'I don't want to do anything else. I want to go back to this very industry and clear my name.'

'But Raghav, you are unnecessarily punishing yourself. Don't do this.'

'Tarana, you don't understand. Let me sort this out my way.'

Tarana could see that the discussion was not going anywhere, so she left Raghav alone.

At dinner, she spoke to him again.

'Your dad wanted to speak to you. Give him a call when you have time.'

Raghav asked Tarana, 'Why don't you take the boys and go to India and spend some time there?'

'Yes, I wanted to spend some time with my parents. But I don't think now is the time.'

'On the contrary, I think now is the time. I need some time to myself. Having you guys around is not helping me concentrate.'

'Are you serious? I don't know what's happened to you.'

'Sitting at home and seeing all of you around me is only adding to my pressure. Only when I'm alone will I be able to concentrate.'

'Okay, fine. If that's what you want.'

After a few weeks, Raghav dropped off Tarana and the boys at JFK and was returning to New Jersey when Harpreet called again. Raghav didn't answer. There was too much on his mind.

Raghav got near Brooklyn Bridge and parked his car. He then walked on the bridge. The last time he had done this was when he had come to the US for the first time. Time had flown by so fast since then. The country and the city had given him everything. But today, he was at a crossroads. He was without a job, had a tarnished reputation and had loans to pay off.

Raghav kept walking on the bridge aimlessly watching other people. Just then he realized that he had missed his Prozac dose. He turned around and walked back to the car, hoping to find some water. Tarana usually stocked the car with everything one could possibly need for a road trip. Luckily, he found a sealed water bottle. He popped the anti-depressant capsule and sat in the car for some time.

As he was parking the car in the garage, he remembered that Tarana had asked him to call his dad about two weeks ago and he'd completely forgotten about it. He decided to call him immediately.

'Hi, papa. How are you doing?'

'I'm fine. Hope you are keeping well. Don't be too worried about your job. You will get one very soon. Tarana told me that she's coming to India. Have they left for Mumbai?'

'Yes, they have. I just dropped them a while back. Tarana will call you when she reaches her parents' house in Mumbai. She was telling me you wanted to speak to me.'

'Oh yes. Nothing very important, just one of those things. You know since retirement I've been thinking about how to make children more aware of our history. I don't think today's children appreciate our ancient history at all. Today's children just want to play video games and watch movies. You remember when you were very small and I was working at the Bhimbetka rock shelters near Bhopal. You were so fascinated by the 30,000-year-old rock paintings that you started drawing them on our house walls. After all these years of working at the Archaeological Survey of India (ASI), I wish I could teach young minds more about our heritage. I was wondering if you have any ideas on how this can be done. I was thinking if we could create an interesting online game that teaches kids our history. It may be useful to them.'

'Ah papa. I don't know. I don't think there's much of a market for these ideas. People are not interested in finding out what happened 1,000 years back.'

'Okay, but do you know anyone who has used technology in the field of archaeology?'

Raghav now sounded irritated.

'Papa, I work in consumer technology and have no interest in what archaeologists do. I suggest you take up the assignment that ASI is offering. I'm sure it will be a good experience.'

'Hmm… Maybe you are right. Let me speak to them,' replied his father concealing his disappointment.

***

Another month passed and still nothing. Raghav even tried to get in touch with the office of Hartmann, the CEO of the Pathbreaker Group, but there was no response. His telephonic interactions with Tarana had also started to dwindle.

One evening, Raghav was tired after surfing through the job sites, when he decided to check his email. He was surprised to see a message from Nafisa, a batchmate from his engineering college days.

'Hi, Raghav! Long time. There are quite a few folks from our batch now in New York and we were planning a get-together on

April 9. Hope you will be able to make it.'

Though Raghav had accepted Nafisa's friend request on Facebook a long time ago, there was hardly any communication between the two. Harpreet was the only batchmate from graduation that he was in touch with. Though he remembered Harpreet mentioning that Nafisa was in Boston, Raghav had never met her. The latest he knew about her was that she ran a data analytics company in Boston, was recently divorced, and had no kids.

In normal circumstances, Raghav may have made the effort to attend the get-together but with his current situation he had absolutely no interest in it.

A couple of days later, Raghav was browsing through the messages on his phone when he came across one from Harpreet.

'Hey, Raghav. We are planning a get-together on 9th April. Hope you'll be able to join. Look forward to seeing you there. Cheers, Harpreet.'

Raghav's assumption that not having Tarana and the kids around would help him concentrate on getting a new job was turning out to be false. The disciplined life that he led as a corporate executive was now a thing of the past. The only semblance of a structured life was thanks to the maid who managed the cooking and the cleaning. But that only helped in organizing the physical world around him. His mind was still in a state of total disarray.

After two weeks, when Raghav was finishing breakfast and getting ready for the meeting with Paul Schuller, the technology head of mobility at RakTech, he saw a meeting request from Nafisa. He was already running late and was very irritated by this distraction. Nonetheless, he quickly clicked on the message.

Howdy Folks,

Time to relive the memories of those good old days.

Don't miss the evening of your life. So, hurry up and accept the invite.

Cheers,

Nafisa

A part of Raghav was telling him that it would be depressing to attend a do where he would probably be the only unemployed person. Another part of him wanted this repeated distraction to end. He was getting late for the meeting and didn't want to lose focus. In his frustration, he clicked the request and it got accepted. He quickly shut down his iPad and rushed out to take the subway.

The meeting did not last long. Paul was kind enough to meet Raghav because they had collaborated together earlier. Though Paul genuinely felt that Raghav would be an asset to his organization, he was candid enough to tell him that the company was not hiring for the next six months.

In the subway, on the way back from the meeting, Raghav opened his iPad to check for any replies from his network. He wanted to check the date and time of the meeting request from Nafisa that he'd accepted.

He read the subject line, 'LOL Evening,' and somehow it felt so typical of Nafisa.

STRIKE THE PIÑATA

Sitting in the New York subway, Raghav looked at the indicator light expectantly, waiting for it to glow and announce the arrival of Astor Place.

Normally on his ride back home, Raghav would be so busy working on his iPad, trying to sort out his emails that he would invariably be the last person to disembark. But today was different. He had nothing much to do, so he just sat there staring blankly waiting for his station.

After a while the light on the indicator panel glowed. It was Astor Place.

Raghav stepped out of the subway carriage and followed the crowd of passengers towards the exit. When he reached the stairs bearing the exit signboard, he stood there looking at it. Suddenly, instead of walking towards the stairs, he turned towards the ticket counter on the right. He was no longer interested in attending the get-together. He took his place in the queue for a ticket back home. He was happy to see that there were only seven to eight people ahead of him. Ten minutes later when the queue did not move people started giving each other annoyed glances.

Raghav saw the first person in the queue walk out, so he stopped him and asked.

'What happened? Didn't you get your ticket?'

'Subways on the line are going to be delayed for the next two hours. Apparently, some technical glitch.'

Raghav shook his head in disgust and cursed his luck. He felt cornered but was left with no choice but to walk out of the Exit.

Though he had lived all these years in New York, this was the first time that Raghav was visiting Astor Place in the East Village area. He reached Alamo Cube, a popular meeting place in East Place, and stopped for a few seconds to admire the simple yet elegant sculpture of a large black cube fixed on one of its edges. A few strangers were enjoying themselves pushing the cube on its edges trying to rotate it on one of its corners.

Raghav walked into the underground gastropub and looked around, hoping to find someone from the group. A young portly manager walked up to him and asked cheerfully, 'Sir, do you have a reservation?'

'Please check for the name Harpreet Singh.'

'Haaarpreet Singg,' said the manager, stretching his name like a child would stretch chewing gum from his mouth.

'Sir, please follow me.'

'I'd prefer a corner table.'

The manager showed Raghav a corner table. Raghav gave a nod of approval and seated himself comfortably around the table. He looked around the pub. It had a cosy rustic charm to it. The air inside had a distinct smell. Raghav couldn't put a finger on it, but it seemed to be a mix of beer and old wooden furniture.

A waiter walked up to Raghav and placed the liquor menu on the table. He looked at Raghav expectantly.

'Hmm ... Give me like five minutes. I'm waiting for a few people.'

Raghav didn't' realize that he had actually turned up quite early.

Looking at the vast selection of craft beers and ciders on the menu, Raghav immediately understood why Harpreet had chosen this place. 'This must be part of Harpreet's mission to try out as many different beers before he dies,' thought Raghav.

The waiter returned in five minutes. Raghav ordered a fresh lime drink.

Raghav found it surreal that so many of his batchmates were in New York at the same time. But then he paused and corrected himself. Actually, there was nothing surreal about the location. For most educated middle-class Indians, the city that never sleeps was always ranked high on the list of must-visit places. Given the fact that several of his college mates were working in the US, there was a higher probability of them meeting in New York than India.

Raghav sat up in his seat and pulled out his phone from the pocket. He logged into Facebook and was about to update his status to 'with batch mates at Jimmy's No. 43 E 7th St, New York' when a familiar voice broke the silence. 'Hey Raghav!' said Harpreet, giving him a pat on his back.

Raghav got up, and they both hugged each other.

'Oye Raghav, can't believe that we're meeting after so long,' said Harpreet.

'You bet! Despite living in the same city for eternity.'

Venky and Aadil joined a little later. Nafisa came in next. Last to join the group were Francis and Shivam.

Nafisa was the only one who had come from outside New York. The rest of them were all in New York, either living in the city permanently or temporarily on work.

Seeing the table fill up, the waiter was back to take the remaining orders.

Harpreet told the waiter, 'Please bring us three pitchers of your best Belgian beer.' And winking at the others, he said with a laugh, 'We'll see if we need more.'

Except Raghav and Nafisa, everybody nodded in unison.

'Looks like Tanker's wife doesn't let him drink. He's making the best of today's opportunity,' teased Nafisa.

'What will you have, Nafisa?' asked Harpreet.

'A mojito with not too much ice would be nice,' replied Nafisa, stressing on the rhyming words.

The waiter looked at Raghav and asked, 'Sir, can I get you another drink?'

Harpreet seized the opportunity and blurted, 'Get him a glass of lassi. He's from Punjab, he drinks only buttermilk.'

Everyone burst out laughing but the waiter seemed utterly confused. The evening had begun on the right note of fun!

People formed groups of two and spent the next thirty minutes discussing their careers and their companies. Raghav participated a bit but was mostly silent. Nafisa was getting bored with the talk and interrupted.

'Guys, this party's getting boring. Let's do something fun.'

Francis protested, 'Nafisa, we're enjoying our beers. Nothing can be more fun than that.'

'C'mon guys. Don't know when we'll meet again. Let's make things interesting,' insisted Nafisa.

'Okay let's hear your "interesting' idea," said Shivam, drawing quotes in the air.

'Okay, so here's the deal. Each of us has to recount an incident from our college days. The incident can be anything. It can be something about your roommate, the canteen, your teacher, your girlfriend. Anything, absolutely anything. It will be nice if it is something funny and interesting and not something boring about how you aced your tests. So, what do you say guys?'

'Hmm. I don't know what was so interesting in those four years,' said Raghav, sounding doubtful.

'Who's in?' asked Nafisa, ignoring Raghav.

The others weren't sure what was expected of them but they nodded their heads nonetheless. Only Raghav shrugged his shoulders and then nodded reluctantly.

'Okay, who'll start first?' asked Aadil excitedly.

'Simple, let's ask the waiter for a beer bottle and spin it. Whoever the bottle points at when it stops, that person has to speak,' said Harpreet.

'C'mon Harpreet, think of something original. Stop copying stuff from chick flicks where the guy ends up kissing the girl in the end after spinning a bottle in a game of Truth or Dare. Think of something original,' said Aadil.

Everybody looked at each other blankly.

'Aadil. You think of something. You were always very creative,' said Nafisa, looking at Aadil.

'Hmm. Let me think. Let me think.'

Aadil turned his head around, looked at the people around him and clapped his hands.

'Got it. All of you give me your mobile phones.'

At first, everyone protested but then they reluctantly handed over their phones to Aadil. Francis was so busy WhatsApping on his phone that Aadil had to snatch the phone from him.

Aadil looked around and then gestured to the waiter.

'Hey Aadil, hope you're not planning to donate our phones to the Salvation Army,' said Venky.

Aadil took one look at Venky's phone and said, 'Nobody in the Salvation Army will take your phone. It's fit only for the dustbin.'

Bob, the waiter, walked up to Aadil, hoping to take another order for drinks.

'My friend, I want you to do us a favour.'

'Yes sir, please tell me.'

'Can you please get me your takeaway bag?' said Aadil, winking at the others.

Soon the waiter was back with a large carry bag.

'Thank you,' said Aadil.

The waiter turned to go back, when Aadil stopped him.

'No wait. I want you to do something more.'

The waiter stood there with a puzzled look, wondering what was coming next.

Aadil took all the mobile phones and put them into the bag.

'My friend, you look like a fun-loving guy to me. So, I thought I would ask you to do something for me. Take this bag of mobiles and keep it with you. When we tell you, you must take the bag with the mobiles to any table and ask one of the guests to put his hand into it and randomly select a mobile phone.'

'Ha ha. Nice idea, Aadil,' said Nafisa raising her hand for a high-five.

'So, the one whose phone gets picked up has to recount an incident. And if he can't do it in five seconds, well, then too bad—he or she will be footing today's bill. You'll be lucky if there are more losers because you'll get to share the bill,' said Aadil, explaining the rules.

Everyone looked at each other.

'Okay everyone, are we on?' asked Aadil, with a grin.

The others had a mixed reaction but they agreed to the game nonetheless.

'Good improvisation, Aadil. So, we are all set to play the game Strike the Piñata,' said Nafisa.

'Strike the Piñata. What the hell is a piñata?' asked Shivam.

'I knew somebody or the other would ask this. A piñata is a decorated figure of an animal containing toys and sweets. It is suspended from a height and broken open by children as part of a celebration, like in a birthday party. Don't you remember, in birthday parties there would be this uncle who gave the birthday boy or girl a stick and he or she would hit this papier mâché bag from which burst out small toys and gifts and all the kids would run to grab them? So, all of you have to strike the piñata of your thoughts and let the memories of those four years fall out,' elaborated Nafisa.

ENGINEERED

Amritsar, Punjab

'What do you want to become when you grow up?' asked one of the mothers at the birthday party, pulling the cheeks of a podgy kid with bright red knickers and a printed half-sleeve shirt.

'Hmm … Tell me.'

The boy's reply was a little late as he was struggling to chew the piece of cake stuffed in his mouth.

Then after some time, Harpreet licked his lips and said confidently, 'Engineer.'

'Hmm… Very good.'

Harpreet knew his answer had hit bullseye. He had heard the word 'engineer' in so many conversations of his parents that he believed that everybody in the world grew up to become engineers. He had often wondered what an engineer actually did; his hunch was that they drove train engines and this seemed like an exciting proposition.

Not bothering to look up after answering the question, Harpreet started devouring the two gulab jamuns that looked like a pair of eyes crying out for his attention.

Vellore, Tamil Nadu

Venkat Srinivas Aiyangar ran up to his father who was sitting on the veranda reading the Sunday paper.

'Appa, appa! When are Kartik and Arvind arriving? I thought they were planning to spend the winter holidays with us.'

'Subhash uncle and his family will be here next week. You better clean up your room so that Kartik and Arvind can stay there. You will be moved to the sofa in our room,' said Venky's father.

'Wow! That will be a lot of fun,' cried Venky. He was thrilled at the prospect of having company for the winter holidays and he didn't mind giving up his room for a few days.

Venky's father, Srinivas Aiyangar, and his uncle, Subhash Iyengar, were brothers but they wrote their surnames differently. One winter, when Subhash returned from the United States, he announced to his family that the correct spelling of their name was 'Iyengar' and not 'Aiyangar.'

So, the Iyengar family arrived at the Aiyangar household with their smart Samsonite suitcases. And, along with various gifts, tumbled stories of the 'developed' world. The living room filled with discussions on how the West was progressing fast, while India was lost in a trap of its own doing.

At dinner, Venky broke the monotonous discussions on East Vs West with his favourite game—the general knowledge quiz.

'What's the capital of Bulgaria?'

Kartik and Arvind pretended not to have even heard the question.

'Tick tick one, tick tick two, tick tick three. Okay, time up. The right answer is Sofia,' said Venky proudly.

'Ok, what is the capital of DRC? I mean, Democratic Republic of Congo.'

Again, there was silence.

'Okay, my last question, then your turn. What is the capital of Vietnam?'

There was still no response.

Kartik and Arvind, who were older than Venky, were beginning to feel a bit embarrassed. They decided to launch a counter fire in the Aiyangar v/s Iyengar battle.

'Okay, explain the Super String theory in physics,' said Kartik confidently.

'I think I have heard this somewhere and I know what it is. It's about rubber bands that can't be snapped,' said Venky excitedly.

Even before Venky could finish, Kartik and Arvind broke into a laughter that reminded Venky of the goons from a crappy Bollywood movie of the Eighties.

'Okay, let me ask you a simpler question. What is the Fibonacci series in mathematics?' asked Arvind.

This time Venky didn't even hazard a guess. He simply asked his mother to pass him the sambar, the unique preparation of a lentil-based vegetable stew .

Srinivas gave his son a long hard stare and said, 'If you want to become an engineer, you must concentrate on physics and maths like your cousins and not general knowledge.'

Thus, Venky was added to the already long list of eleven engineers from the Aiyangar clan.

Pune, Maharashtra

Bhushan Singh did washing, ironing and other odd jobs for the residents of Narmada colony in Pune. He dreaded Saturdays as it meant going to the Siddiqui household.

The Siddiqui household was a joint family and the patriarch, Irfan Siddiqui, ran a thriving trading business. His three sons lived together with him. For Bhushan, going to the Siddiqui household meant dragging his son Narender along, as there was always quite a lot of work in their house. Narender was more interested in playing marbles than helping his father in his work. However, the challenge of dragging his son paled in front of his biggest challenge—Nafisa, Irfan Siddiqui's grand-daughter.

One day, the youngest daughter-in-law of the family, Mrs. Siddiqui, was busy with the usual household chores when Bhushan made his way into their house.

'Bhushan bhaiyya, good you came early today. I need to go to the market. Here are six bundles. Please try to give our bundle and the first-floor bundle before the weekend,' said Mrs. Siddiqui.

'Nafisa! Nafisa!' shouted Mrs Siddiqui. 'Please help bhaiyya.'

In came Nafisa with the TV remote in her hand. She took one glance at all the bundles and said sternly, 'Start.'

Bhushan opened all the bundles and out fell clothes in all colours, shapes and sizes. Even before he could tie the last bundle, Nafisa shouted, 'Mummy, the amount for this week is 467 minus twenty-three from the last time, which bhaiyya owes us. So, the final amount is 444.'

Nafisa was not yet finished.

'Mummy, bhaiyya is charging the same for ironing half-sleeve and full-sleeve shirts. Shouldn't they be different?'

Bhushan and his son looked at each other as if somebody had put coal fire on their backs.

Bhushan was quick to respond, 'No, Nafisa baby. It takes the same effort to iron both.'

Nafisa looked at him and shook her head in disagreement. 'We also need to deduct fifty rupees penalty for burning papa's shirt collar last week. So, the final amount is 394. I'm going to watch TV now.'

Nafisa walked away with a smile and the TV remote in her hand.

Bhushan could never get the math right. So, he was amazed that a seven-year-old girl could total the amount in a jiffy and also remember the sum he owed the family.

Narender looked at his father and said, 'Let's go papa, no point rechecking. Nafisa baby is a computer.'

Jaipur, Rajasthan

Shivam's father, Rajendra Bhatti, returned late one evening after completing the electrical fittings at an apartment in Jaipur's posh suburb, Vaishali Nagar.

His wife Jayanti was waiting for him with his usual dinner. Sitting on the floor, eating his dinner, Rajendra could hear the sound of the TV playing in the next room.

'What time did Shivam return from school?' asked Rajendra.

'He came back early today,' replied Jayanti.

'Hmm… Why?'

'He was saying there were hardly any teachers in school today.'

'I'm getting concerned about his studies. He thinks he's intelligent but actually he doesn't realize that most of the students in his class are morons. In three years, school will get over and he will have to apply to colleges. If he doesn't study in a good place, we will have another electrician in the house. I don't want him to become an electrician like me. He should become an engineer.'

'Yes, you are right,' said Jayanti, agreeing with her husband.

'I will speak to my brother Yogesh tomorrow. I will ask him to call Shivam to Delhi. If he stays with him, he will get the right guidance and hopefully make something out of his life,' said Rajendra.

Calcutta, West Bengal

Aadil Contractor and Sandeep Ahuja were staring blankly at the blackboard. Their ninth-grade economics teacher, Mr Roy, had completed the demand-and-supply graph. They were secretly praying for the peon's hand to slip and ring the bell ten minutes early. But that was not to be. Finally, when the school bell went off, the children sprinted like horses on a racetrack.

'Hey Sandeep, let's go to the washroom and then to the canteen. This economics class has totally fried my brain,' said Aadil, as he rushed towards the washroom.

Sandeep, who was standing next to Aadil's urinal, relieving himself, said, 'You must come to my house this weekend. I've a lot of stuff to show you. I've got new video games, a new watch and three new sweatshirts. There's also a big box of Toblerone, which I'm dying to open.'

Aadil loved the idea of spending an afternoon at Sandeep's house, playing video games and gorging on junk food.

'My uncle will be going back to the US soon. This time, I've asked him to bring a remote-control glider,' said Sandeep.

'So, is your uncle also a businessman like your dad?'

'No. He's a software engineer working for IBM.'

'Wow!' said Aadil, zipping up his pants.

Panjim, Goa

Mark Cardinho had three passions in life—eating prawn pickles, playing the mouth organ and walking on Goa's beaches. His job as a manager in many of Goa's hotels gave him the opportunity to indulge amply in all his pastimes. But this also meant moving houses a lot, which his wife Nancy hated. She longed for a stable life but their children, Jude and Francis, loved it every time they moved homes.

Mark's Sunday morning ritual included taking the boys for a walk in the beach and a quick dip in the sea. Jude was obsessed with collecting pebbles and every week he carried back enough of them to attract a sound hollering from his mother.

Unlike Jude, Francis had to be dragged out of the bed. His interests lay in the three Ms—mathematics, models and Monopoly. Since grade five he had developed such a strong love for mathematics that every academic year he ended up completing his math syllabus well ahead of time. In his free time, Francis also built cardboard models of World War II planes and antique cars.

It was a regular Sunday morning when Mark walked into the boys' room. As usual, Mark found Jude getting ready for the walk, while Francis was sitting on his bed with cardboard pieces scattered all over.

'Get up, boys! We are already late. After the walk, I need to get the scooter fixed,' said Mark.

That morning, the beach looked clean and the air had a slight chill in it. The three of them started their brisk walk along the seashore. After a while, Mark walked towards his regular tea stall and sat down with his newspaper. Jude followed him with a bag of pebbles. Mark started to read his newspaper, while Jude was busy removing the dirt from his collection.

Mark continued reading his paper and sipping tea, hoping Francis would join them soon. But there was no sign of Francis. He waited for another ten minutes and then panicked.

He started running towards the shore. He looked around and couldn't find Francis anywhere. He walked about 100 meters towards the shore when his eye caught a glimpse of a figure sitting on the sand.

As he got closer, he could recognize Francis kneeling on the sand with a stick in his hand. Mark walked up to Francis and stood silently behind him. He noticed that Francis was scribbling something on the sand. He bent closer to see what Francis was scribbling. They looked like random figures. But when he stared at them for long, he noticed they were actually a series of numbers.

Francis was scribbling a long series of numbers separated by mathematical symbols denoting addition, subtraction and division. Francis was challenging himself to calculate the answer before the next wave wiped out the numbers.

THE DEVIL AND THE DEEP SEA

'It's a Google Nexus,' said the waiter, announcing it as if he was a nurse announcing the birth of a new born baby.

This brought a round of applause from the table.

'This is crap,' said Harpreet, putting down his glass of beer. 'I'm not tipping this guy.'

'Your time's starting, bro,' reminded Aadil.

'Okay guys, here's goes the story of Harpreet in the hostel,' said Harpreet wiping the beer off his lips.

***

The smell of parathas being cooked wafted through the air. Joginder Singh Babbar, the canteen owner at Mathewson Technical College, looked at Dheela, his second-in-command and shouted, 'The new batch of students have begun to arrive. Get everything ready quickly. We'll have a lot of students and parents eating today. Quick! Clean the tables. If I see even a single fly on the table, I'll kick you straight back to your village.'

All the waiters burst out laughing. But one look at Babbar's face and they realized he meant business so they quickly got back to work.

Looking down from the second floor of the hostel, Alok said to Ashraf, 'Look, the new batch of chickens is arriving.'

'Then let's plan the barbeque tonight. What do you say?' asked Ashraf.

***

Raghav and Harpreet were happy that they had been able to persuade the warden to allocate them adjacent rooms. They quickly dumped their stuff and hurried to the hostel mess for lunch before any of the seniors saw them.

The two boys had met at a coaching institute that had helped them clear the engineering entrance exam. As luck would have it, they both made it to the same engineering college. Together, they were ready to embark upon the four-year engineering course.

At the lunch table, dusting the wheat flour from his chapattis, Harpreet told Raghav, 'When I finished filling out the hostel forms, I saw a group of seniors. They looked like they could rag us.'

Raghav listened without lifting his head. He continued to look for paneer particulates in his matar paneer.

'But I'm telling you, I'm not going to let these guys rag me. It's not allowed and I won't let it happen. This is bullshit. We didn't crack such a tough exam to be ragged by these buggers. I will not accept anything in the name of ragging,' Harpreet went on and on.

Raghav looked at Harpeet. He could see the confidence oozing out of him.

Harpreet continued, 'I can't understand how ragging is still allowed in hostels. This is absolute rubbish. We have to stand up to these seniors and they will back off. If things go out of hand, I won't think twice before complaining about them. In fact, these guys are cowards. They think they can mess with us. Hell, they can't!'

Raghav and Harpreet looked at their watches and realized it was time for the induction session. They grabbed their bags and ran towards the lecture halls.

At midnight sharp, the silence of the hostel corridor was disturbed. Raghav got up from his bed struggling to make out what it was. The sound was a mix of a dozen slippers running on the floor and that of room doors being banged. He was shaken. The barbeque had started.

Raghav switched on the light and stepped out of his room heavy-eyed. Anant Hegde, his neighbour, also walked out with a bewildered expression on his face and said, 'What's happening? What's all this ruckus? Why are people coming out of their rooms?'

The barrage of questions from Anant jolted Raghav out of his sleep. Before he could answer, he spotted something strange in Anant's appearance.

'Dude! Where are your pyjamas?' asked Raghav, with a surprised expression.

Anant answered coolly, 'I'm more comfortable sleeping in just a kurta (night shirt).'

'Hmm. But I hope you don't want to land up like this in front of the seniors. I hope you get the drift.'

'Oh yeah, yeah. I get it. Let me quickly change.'

By now, all the juniors had assembled in the senior's hostel, dressed in different night clothes. Some in shorts, some in pyjamas, and some others in whatever they could get hold of. The only thing common was the puzzled expression on their faces. The corridor resembled a concentration camp scene from a World War II movie.

All the juniors were asked to assemble in a senior's room and strip. Then they had to introduce themselves.

Most of them started with 'My name is…' and ended with 'I'm from…' Only one or two of them tried to break the monotony.

'Hi, I'm Saahil, Saahil Motwani,' said a voice in confident accented English.

The guy next in line was about to start when one of the seniors interrupted him and looked at Sahil.

'Hmm… So, Mr James Bond, why don't you show us some stunts.'

Saahil stood there with his head down.

'Get into your Aston Martin, drive around the hostel floor for twenty minutes and come back.'

Saahil didn't know what to do.

'Start your car.'

Saahil then lowered his body to get into a seating position and made the sound of an engine revving up.

'Now, somebody please open the door for Mr Bond,' the senior said.

One of the students sheepishly opened the 'door' and Saahil was on his way in his imaginary car.

The seniors burst out laughing at the sight. A senior shouted out to Saahil. 'Mr Bond, make sure your car doesn't break down on the way.'

The introductions were only half done when there was a kick on the door. The door flung open with a loud bang.

Three seniors from the penultimate year batch walked straight into the room, looking strangely at whatever was happening. Shiva, one of the three seniors, smiled at the group of juniors and asked, 'Why are you all standing with your heads down like newly-married brides?'

Shiva was unlike how an engineer is often visualized to be. He was around 6 feet 3 inches tall, rotund, with dark red lips as a result of constantly chewing on beetle leaves. He wore a tight tee shirt, and a shiny bracelet hung loosely from his wrist.

The manner in which he spoke and his abrupt entry onto the scene made the juniors feel a bit relieved. But nobody dared to lift their heads to say anything.

'Sorry for the interruption, ladies. There's an emergency and we need your help,' said Shiva, with a serious expression and a rather gruff voice.

Shiva looked at his friend Rajan and then at the freshers and said, 'Which of you new brides can ride a bike?'

A few freshers sniggered at this, but they controlled themselves quickly.

Only three students, including Harpreet, raised their hands. Raghav thought it stupid of Harpreet to choose this occasion to reveal his 'special' skill to the world.

Rajan and Shiva then started surveying the juniors who could ride the bike. One was a skinny guy, one was a short chap and the other was a tall, well-built Sikh boy.

Rajan and Shiva looked at Harpreet and then at each other and nodded their heads. Rajan looked at Harpeet and said, 'Okay, so you will go. Take our bike and money. Go to the theka outside the campus, buy a crate of beer and bring it to the hostel. Simple.'

When Harpreet heard this, his eyes widened and a worried look enveloped his face. Raghav could see that Harpreet was about to explode.

Harpreet straightened himself and, in a respectful voice, said, 'Sir, which brand of beer should I get?'

Raghav couldn't believe what he had heard. He stared long and hard at Harpreet. Harpreet must have felt his eyes on him so gave him a fleeting glance and then walked up to Rajan to take the bike keys and the money.

Harpreet felt a little braver now. He confidently asked Shiva, 'Sir, can I take Raghav with me?'

In the corridor, Raghav kept yelling at Harpreet, 'You idiot! I thought you were going to refuse. You chickened out, man! Big time! Now, we are stuck with this crazy task. You should have kept your mouth shut.'

Harpreet said coolly, 'Relax, I can handle this.'

Harpreet started the bike. He was about to leave the hostel gate, when both Raghav and Harpreet looked at the list of Dos and Don'ts painted in bold letters on the hostel wall. Their eyes immediately locked onto the eighth pointer: *Students caught drinking or possessing alcohol in the hostel premises will be rusticated with immediate effect.*

A shiver ran down their spine. They realized they had been conned.

The hostel guard was woken up by the sound of the bike and

stood up to open the gate.

'Where are you going so late at night?' asked the old hostel guard, Kishan Lall.

'Nothing. Nothing. We are just going out,' replied Raghav sheepishly.

Harpreet and Raghav asked for directions from someone on the road and headed towards the theka on the highway. It was a good five kilometres from the campus and remained open throughout the night to cater to truck drivers.

Harpreet stood at the counter and hesitantly asked for a crate of Kingfisher beer.

Raghav asked Harpreet, 'Do you really think we have to do this? This is too risky. Getting caught can land us in serious trouble.'

'You've got a point, but…'

From the manner in which Harpreet emphasized the word 'but,' Raghav understood that Harpreet's mind was already drawing a picture of Shiva towering over him, ready to wring his neck.

Raghav said to the man at the counter, 'Put six Coke bottles also in the box.'

The easy part was done, the tough part of getting the beers inside remained. During the ride back to the hostel, Raghav kept presenting various options to Harpreet on how to dodge the guard.

Kishan Lall was fast asleep when he heard someone shouting. He quickly woke up and ran out of the gate. He saw a bike and one of the freshers who had left the hostel an hour ago on a bike shouting wildly.

As Kishan Lall approached the bike, he saw the other fresher lying on the ground, his body shaking vigorously.

Harpreet looked at the guard with a confused look, 'Bhaiyya, please see what has happened to him. He… he… just starting shaking and fell off the bike. I don't know what happened. Looks like an epilepsy attack.'

The guard took one look at Raghav lying on the ground shaking strangely and said, 'You are right, this is an epilepsy attack. But don't worry, I know to tackle this. I've seen enough of these things in my village.'

The guard quickly took out his worn-out boot and shoved it in front of Raghav's nose, forcing him to smell it. According to Kishan Lall, this was the ultimate treatment for a person under an epilepsy attack.

Raghav started shaking his body even more vigorously, unable to tolerate the smell from the old shoe. Harpreet understood his dilemma and shouted, 'No! No! This is will not work. This will make matters worse. We need to get a doctor quickly.'

But Kishan Lall was adamant, 'Trust me, this will work.' He pushed Harpreet's hand aside and took his shoe towards Raghav's face again. Seeing that Kishan Lall was hell-bent on trying out his 'tried and tested' technique, Harpreet was left with no choice but to snatch the shoe and swing it away. The shoe landed a couple of meters away.

Harpreet turned to Kishan Lall and ordered, 'Now, go find a doctor before this guy dies.'

The guard hopped on one leg, picked up his shoe, and ran towards the university dispensary.

Harpreet patted Raghav and said, 'Keep shaking. He may come back any time.'

He then went towards the nearby ditch and lifted the box with the beer bottles and started running towards the hostel building.

Harpreet's sprint was nothing short of Daniel Carter's run on the rugby pitch. He held onto the box and ran as though winning the world cup depended on him. Panting and sweating profusely, Harpreet completed the run, dropped the box behind the hostel's main door and ran back to Raghav before the guard came back with a doctor.

Both Raghav and Harpreet carried the box to the hostel terrace to find Shiva, Rajan and the gang devouring buckets of butter chicken and paneer tikka. When the gang saw the box with beers, there was loud clapping and cheering.

News of the arrival of the bottles travelled fast and soon the terrace was full of students from other batches too.

Harpreet was finishing his third beer, when Shiva and a few other seniors walked up to him.

Shiva looked at Raghav and Harpreet and said, 'Harpreet the Tanker and Raghav the Shaker! Welcome to the best four years of your life. Cheers!'

Shiva looked at Raghav and said, 'Where's your beer?'

Raghav looked at them straight and replied confidently, 'Sir, I don't drink alcohol. I'm from Punjab, I only drink lassi.'

Shiva and Rajan burst out laughing and clinked their beer bottles with a loud shout, 'Cheers to Raghav and his lassi!'

Everyone went back to enjoying the terrace party. Raghav and Harpeet were talking about their lucky escape when they overheard one of the guys standing next to them saying, 'I'd gone downstairs to take a leak. There I saw the campus doctor and the guard standing in the corridor. I wonder what happened. Did somebody fall sick?'

Harpreet and Raghav looked at each other and gulped down their drinks.

***

'So, now I know how you got your name,' said Nafisa. 'Okay, who's next?'

Harpreet indicated to the waiter who smiled and took the bag of mobiles to an unsuspecting table occupied by a couple of young college girls who were merrily giggling and enjoying their evening.

'Excuse me, ma'am,' the waiter said to a girl.

The girl stopped what she was saying and looked at him.

'Ma'am, can I request you to put your hand in the bag and pull out a mobile phone?'

One of the girls looked at the waiter and asked, 'Have we won a lucky draw?"

'No ma'am. You see the table there. The folks there are playing a game and the next person's turn to speak comes when a mobile phone is drawn.'

'Wow. This is so cool,' said another girl looking that the group of Indians.

The first girl put her hand into the bag and pulled out an old iP-hone 4 and handed it to the waiter.

The waiter waved the phone at their table.

Venky was embarrassed by his outdated phone and flashed a sheepish thumbs-up sign at the girls.

TWF 177

On a cold winter evening, Venky and Aadil decided to watch a movie at Bharat Talkies, a dilapidated cinema theatre in the city. The movie didn't matter to them as long as they could idle away a few hours and binge on hot masala dosas with rasam and sambhar on their way back.

After the movie and a heavy dinner, they were walking up the hostel staircase recalling a funny scene from the B-grade movie Honeymoon of the Devils, when they took a peek into Harpreet's room. The room was crowded with people but there was an eerie silence. The usual banter, which went on till the wee hours of the morning sometimes, was missing. Harpreet was staring at a sheet of paper as if it was a letter from the US Consulate rejecting his visa to America. Venky and Aadil instantly knew it was the results of Prof Shantanu Dey's mid-term test.

'Who's the bloody idiot who has brought this marksheet to the hostel?' cursed Venky. 'Surely it could have waited till the morning.'

Giving a whack on Shashank's head, Harpreet said, 'Mr Shashank Trivedi, great grandson of Albert Einstein, had nothing better to do in the evening than walk to the department and note down everyone's marks. Next time, please just note down your marks; we'll worry about ours.'

None of what Harpreet said had any effect on Shashank. He just sat there staring at all of them like Arnold Schwarzenegger from Terminator II.

Venky took a look at the sheet and started searching for his name. Most of the marks were in single digits; it was as if Prof Dey was mocking them by creating a pattern from his phone number. One of the numbers caught his eye. It was 0.5. A solitary decimal number among whole numbers. When he glanced at the name, he was horrified to see the two letters. VA. For Venky Aiyangar. He couldn't believe it. He had actually got a measly 0.5—the lowest mark in the class.

Suddenly, Venky latched onto a thought that had been brewing in his mind for long. 'Chuck engineering, prepare for your MBA,' he thought to himself, thinking that a career in business management would be more up his alley. Not only would a management degree give him much more financial security, but it would also boost his prospects for marriage, felt Venky. He knew that a number of people in his family were boasting about having found an MBA groom for their daughters.

Venky spent the next couple of days speaking to a few seniors. He found out about a coaching institute in the city. The training institute for the Common Admission Test, popularly called CAT, was a good seventeen kilometres away; one could either take a state roadways bus and get squashed in it or ride a scooter or bike to get there. Though the bus was definitely the cheaper option, it would certainly ruin his already low 'coolness' quotient in the batch.

The very next weekend, Venky, along with Aadil, went home. Venky wanted to convince his father to let him take his scooter to the hostel. He knew it would not be easy as the scooter was his father's prized possession and Venky's track record of being responsible for things was not very great. However, at the breakfast table, Venky mustered up the courage and tentatively broached the subject with his father. After answering his father's questions in the increasing order of difficulty as in the popular television show Who Wants to Be a Millionaire? Venky was given the key to the 1982 Lambretta. As he sat on the scooter, Venky felt like a pilot who had earned his wings and was ready to fly his first MIG-29 sortie. Well, the scooter was not an MIG-29. In fact, even calling it a biplane would have been an exaggerated compliment to the vintage vehicle.

Venky had made Aadil his partner in crime and had coaxed him into riding along with him on the scooter to the college hostel.

Venky rode the scooter and reached Aadil's house at 5a.m. to find Aadil and his parents eagerly waiting for him. Aadil's mother had made sure that Aadil was wearing all the woollens in the house that she could get hold of.

Seeing Aadil in that state, Venky couldn't help remarking, 'Don't you want to bring a quilt as well?' Aadil's mother heard this and retorted, 'Venkat beta, it will be very cold in the highway. If you want, I can give you a spare muffler.'

Venky replied sheepishly, 'No, aunty. I think I can manage.'

Aadil's excitement quickly melted when he saw the scooter.

Venky was keen to show off that although the scooter looked old, it could start like a bike. He gave it one kick and waited. Nothing happened. He gave it another kick, again nothing happened. Finally, he had to tilt the scooter towards him to kick-start it. After seeing this, Venky hoped that Aadil wouldn't change his mind.

Aadil gave Venky an annoyed look and sat down on the pillion seat with a bag of eatables packed by his mother. Aadil looked at Venky and said, 'I don't think this thing can make it through 350 kilometres.' Venky too was skeptical about it but he knew he had to sound confident for the success of Operation Scooter Delivery. So, without a pause, he blurted out, 'What rubbish! This contraption may look old but it's nothing short of gold.'

Looking at the two speed away on the 'contraption', Aadil's parents said a silent prayer and went back into their house.

Riding out of the congested roads of Delhi onto the highway gave Venky and Aadil a new lease of freedom. Though this was Venky's first time on a highway, he rode like a veteran. They rode past the light morning fog that hovered over lush mustard fields and numerous dhabas. Venky rode for over an hour before handing over the scooter to Aadil. Initially, Aadil was apprehensive but slowly became confident and briskly overtook tractors, bikes and the odd slow-moving car.

Their plan was to stop for breakfast in the next town. So, Aadil decided to give the Lambretta a throttle. The scooter tried its best to compete against the other vehicles, but it simply didn't have the legs.

All of a sudden, Venky heard the sound of a motorbike behind him and shouted to Aadil to give way. Aadil could barely understand what Venky was saying and tried to look in the rear-view mirror.

Aadil shouted, 'I don't see any bike.' By then, Venky had also turned his head and realized there was nothing. Just then, Aadil slammed the brakes. 'The bloody silencer has gone kaput! I told you this thing won't go very far. Now you'll buy me breakfast.' Aadil revved up the scooter but quickly cut off the engine as the sound from the broken silencer was deafening.

With a look of embarrassment on his face, Venky took the scooter from Aadil and rode it in the direction of the nearby town. They were lucky that even before they reached the town, they spotted a mechanic by the side of the road.

The mechanic started fixing the scooter. When he was done, he got up to say, 'You are very brave to ride this scooter all the way from Delhi.'

Though this incident shook them up for a moment, the boys were relieved that they were able to eventually get the scooter going. Venky and Aadil continued to ride and stopped only occasionally to give their aching body some rest and drink cups of piping hot chai from the roadside vendors.

When they were about twenty kilometres from the college, Venky increased the speed of the scooter. He wanted to reach the hostel before dinner to avoid the Lambretta getting too much attention. The scooter was now on reserve fuel but Venky and Aadil thought they would be able to make it in time.

They had hardly cruised for a couple of kilometres when the scooter started sputtering. They both looked at each other. They knew they had run out of fuel. Venky tilted the scooter and started it again. They rode for another kilometre and then the same thing happened. They did these six more times before the scooter came to an absolute standstill.

Aadil said to Venky, 'We'll need petrol now. Let me take a lift from someone and go to a petrol pump.'

Aadil got to know from a passer-by on the street that the nearby petrol station was about a kilometre away.

Aadil stood by the road and started asking passers-by for a ride, while Venky continued his efforts to start the scooter.

A couple of cars and bikes passed by but nobody stopped. Aadil was getting mighty frustrated and decided to make one last ditch effort. Just then, he saw a motorcycle speeding towards them at 100 kilometres an hour. Aadil jumped on the road and started waving wildly at the bike.

Seeing the two students in trouble, the rider decided to stop and the bike screeched to a halt.

Aadil was thankful the biker had stopped. He pleaded with him, 'Brother, can you please drop me at the nearest petrol station?' The biker nodded his head and asked him to sit on the pillion seat.

Aadil was just about to sit on the bike when Venky, who was oblivious to what was going on, managed to start the scooter. He looked back and shouted at Aadil, 'Quickly get on the scooter or it will stop again.' Aadil didn't know what to do. He was confused whether to sit on the bike or the scooter.

Aadil had half a mind to sit on the bike, but Venky wouldn't stop shouting. Aadil turned around, rushed towards Venky and sat on the pillion seat. The biker was livid with anger. But instead of an explanation, Aadil only had an angelic smile to offer. Without wasting any time, Venky gave the scooter a throttle and sped past the biker.

The frustrated biker gave the boys his choicest expletives and overtook them, shaking his fist at them.

Venky and Aadil couldn't control their laughter when they finally reached the petrol station. After filling petrol, they stretched their legs one last time and were on their way again. When they entered the hostel gate, they were relieved to see that no one was standing in the parking lot. They quickly parked the scooter, picked up their bags and started walking towards their rooms.

All of a sudden, they heard footsteps followed by laughter. They recognized the voices of their seniors.

Raghav was the first one to see Venky and Aadil standing next to the scooter. He walked up to the scooter, gave it one hard look and laughed out aloud. 'How the hell did you manage to get this museum piece all the way from Delhi? This thing looks like it was built in the 1930s.'

Vivek, another senior, chipped in sarcastically, 'Guys, how many bullock carts overtook you on the way, eh?'

The third senior, Rajat, looked at the scooter and remarked, 'TWF 177 is a very weird number, but if you jumble the alphabets around it does become quite interesting.'

The seniors laughed loudly and asked them both to join them for dinner.

***

'Venky, where's your scooter these days?' asked Aadil, 'Have you sold that piece of junk or do you still have it?'

'No, I haven't sold it. I intend to give it to you as a present on your 50th birthday,' said Venky.

'Actually, you may want to give it to another of your friends as a present,' remarked Aadil.

'Ha ha! I know whom you are referring to. Let me tell you the second part of this story,' said Venky.

APPLIED MATH

One day, when Aadi and Venky were on their way to the tutorial classes, Aadil complained to Venky, 'Man! your scooter is a fish. We barely make it for three classes and the tank empties. I've already exhausted my funds for the month. At this rate, I'm going to be broke in no time.'

Venky replied with an I-care-a-damn expression, 'So, what do you want me to do? Buy you a bike?'

Aadil replied, 'I wish you could do that. But I don't want you to sell your kidney just yet. I've got a better idea.'

'Bark.'

'Distribute cost by roping in a third person.'

'You're right, but how do we get someone else to join us? I don't see anybody in the batch interested in doing an MBA. And why would anyone start preparing so early?'

'Don't worry. We'll soon find one'

A couple of days later, Aadil and Venky were at the hostel mess. They were having dinner when Prashant came and sat across them.

Aadil looked at Venky and winked. Venky didn't understand what was about to happen but he was ready to play along.

Prashant smirked at the two boys, 'So guys, how's your MBA prep going?'

Venky tried to appear cool as he said, 'Early days. Let's see how it goes.'

'I was wondering why you guys started preparations so early. Aren't you guys going to the branch near Central Market? That's a good twenty kilometres from the university. Isn't it?'

Aadil had finished his dinner and was about to leave. 'Venky, don't keep eating as if you haven't eaten in a month. Finish quickly. Don't we have to take down notes from the book I borrowed?'

Venky looked a bit confused and said, 'Yeah right. Whose notebook did you bring?'

Aadil replied confidently, 'Shalini's.'

Venky looked even more confused now. 'Who is Shalini?'

Aadil twitched his eyebrow.

'The girl who has come from the US.'

Venky got the drift and nodded.

Aadil looked at Venky and said, 'Well, I need to leave now.'

Prashant seemed a little interested when he said, 'So, does your coaching centre consist of only engineers or are there others as well?'

Venky gobbled his dinner as he spoke, 'There are a lot of engineers but a decent number from the girls' College of Commerce.'

Prashant's eyes lit up.

By then Aadil had gone up to his room. He was lying on his bed when he heard a knock on the door. He knew it was Venky. So, he quickly jumped onto his bed and opened a few notebooks.

'Yes! Coming.'

Aadil opened the door and found Venky and Prashant standing on the corridor.

Venky came straight to the point, 'Hey Aadil, do you think my scooter can handle a triply?'

Aadil looked at Venky with a knowing smile and said, 'Hmm, I think it will be difficult. It's a very old machine.'

Prashant interjected the conversation, 'I thought I'll pool in with you guys and check out the coaching centre.'

'Venky's scooter's is pretty old. So, I don't know if it can handle three people.'

Prashant was insistent, 'Don't worry. If there's any maintenance hassle, I don't mind paying for it.'

Aadil and Venky looked at other each. They could immediately picture themselves using their additional savings to devour jalebis at Lucky Sweet Shop and watch more movies.

Aadil pretended to finally relent. 'Okay, let's try it for two weeks and see how it goes. In fact, you should join us tomorrow itself. We'll go together for the classes.'

'Cool! So, see you tomorrow,' said Prashant and left the room feeling mighty chuffed with himself.

Prashant had only taken a few paces when Aadil went after him.

'Just one last thing. We pool in money for the scooter in advance. So, please bring the money tomorrow.'

Prashant looked at him and simply nodded.

Aadil went back into the room, looked at Venky and burst out laughing so loudly that Venky had to nearly strangle him.

The next morning, the boy's hostel was abuzz with the activity of the boys desperately trying to get ready for the 8.30 a.m. class.

Venky was tucking in his shirt, combing his hair and chewing stuffed parathas all at the same time. Just then, Aadil and Prashant barged into the room to get the keys. They picked up the scooter key from the table and ran out quickly to start the scooter.

Venky could hear the sound of Aadil and Prashant trying to start the scooter with no success. He was getting a thrill out of seeing them, especially Prashant, struggle with the scooter. The vintage scooter would start with a single kick only once in a blue moon and today was not that day.

Venky ambled down the stairs humming a tune and took charge of his scooter. He tilted the vehicle and gave it a hard, full-blooded kick. TWF 177 roared to life with a cloud of thick blue smoke.

Venky shouted, 'Get on it quickly. She's ready for take-off.'

Aadil and Prashant quickly jumped on the pillion seat, with Venky trying hard to prevent the scooter from doing a wheelie.

The students eating breakfast on the benches outside the canteen turned around to see a vintage scooter with three students hurtling towards them.

One of them got up and shouted, 'Get out of the way, before these idiots mow us down.'

***

'Now that explains why Prashant never cleared CAT. He must have been so busy devising a plan to recover the money he spent on your scooter that he would have forgotten all about the exam,' said Shivam with a hearty laugh.

'So, who's next?' asked Harpreet.

Aadil turned around and waived at the waiter.

The waiter understood and took the bag to one of the tables.

He then returned to their table with an iPhone 6 in a silver emoji bling cover.

It was Nafisa's.

JUST DO IT

'Why does it take forever for the canteen to serve a simple thing like a samosa. Professors spend hours teaching us about efficiency but they never look at how the processes around them can be improved,' moaned Nafisa.

'Men are from Mars and women are from Venus but which planet are you from Nafisa? The canteen is the only place where things are leisurely and you want to change even that. Slow down,' said Harpreet with a laugh.

In walked Aadil looking like a scarecrow, wearing an oversized T-shirt branded with his favourite rock band Aerosmith, and waving a brochure in his hand.

Flinging the brochure on the table, Aadil said, 'Guys, read this.'

Nafisa picked up the brochure and quickly glanced at it. She found it very interesting.

'Software development contest. Hmm, seems like a good opportunity to try out some coding skills. The only hitch is putting together a working programme in two-and-a-half weeks in between class tests,' said Nafisa, with a tinge of disappointment.

'I think if we come up with a good concept, we stand a good chance. I'm going for it. Who else is in?' asked Aadil.

'There's no harm trying. I'm also in,' said Nafisa excitedly.

Before the others started pressurizing him, Harpreet quickly picked up his bag and walked out. Nafisa and Aadil were looking at Harpreet when the canteen waiter came in with the samosas. Everyone picked up a samosa each and started walking towards the class.

Nafisa walked up to Harpreet and said, 'You are easily the best coder in the class. We'll need you if we want to win this.'

Aadil too supported Nafisa. 'Yes Harpreet, we'll need you.'

With an uninterested expression on his face, Harpreet said, 'I'm not sure I have the time, plus this semester is very tough.'

The three of them went into the lecture hall and took their seats. Nafisa sat in the first row, Aadil in the middle row and Harpeet right at the back.

After class, everyone rushed to the water coolers before the next class started. Harpeet leisurely walked up to Nafisa and Aadil, who were discussing their entry in the software programming contest.

Handing over a few sheets, Harpreet said to them, 'I've put together a concept for automating a pharmacy. What do you guys think?'

Nafisa jumped with joy and nearly hugged Harpreet.

Nafisa looked at the sheets and read through the details. 'I think this is a great idea. Let's start working on it. I will meet the guy who runs the college pharmacy and understand the pharmacy processes so that our software is authentic.'

Aadil and Harpreet were impressed with Nafisa's enthusiasm.

The three of them knew it would be difficult to balance course work along with coding for this event but they had no choice. Harpreet took the lead as the idea was his and he was also the best coder among the three.

As none of them owned a computer or a laptop and the university's computer centre was not open in the evenings, they were left with no option but to look at computer facilities outside the university.

'Bright Future Computer Institute' was an upcoming computer learning centre outside the university. Since the centre was fairly new, the owner was happy to rent out his extra computers.

Every day after class, the three of them took an autorickshaw and went to the computer centre to work on the project. Sometimes, Aadil borrowed Venky's scooter. They divided the work among themselves. Harpreet was the technical lead and did most of the coding. Nafisa played the role of a business analyst by translating the processes of the pharmacy into algorithms. Aadil did a bit of everything but focused mainly on testing the application as it was getting built. He also was the odd-job man responsible for ordering the samosas and tea, negotiating with the autorickshaw guys and coaxing the attendant in college to keep the computer lab open for longer.

There was healthy camaraderie among the three and they were happy to take on each other's responsibilities when the need arose.

As the days went by, the pressure of the project started to show on the three. There were several arguments. Some of them were quite heated: what features to put in, how the screen should look, whether the project was worth their effort, etc.

One day, Harpreet and Nafisa were busy discussing a business scenario, when Aadil walked in looking worried.

'There's good news. Professor Murthy has decided to give two tests in the next three days,' announced Aadil sarcastically.

'What? Why?' shrieked Nafisa, unable to contain her anger and disappointment.

The last six days were very crucial for their software project as they had to integrate and test all the components they had built.

'Professor Murthy is going on leave for three weeks. So, he wants to conduct all the tests before his holiday. There's only a day's gap and there are three units for each of the tests. My first test didn't go well, so these two tests are very critical for me,' said Aadil, indirectly indicating that he would not be able to contribute towards the project for the next few days.

Harpreet was silent all this while. He tried to put up a brave front.

'The tests finish by Friday, so we have Saturday to finish the project and then we have to submit it on Sunday before 8a.m. That should be cool,' said Harpreet with confidence.

Nafisa and Aadil were impressed with Harpreet's ability to absorb the shock.

'So, let's study for the tests till Friday and use the weekend to work on the project. What do you guys say?' said Nafisa, laying out the plan for the coming days.

'I guess we don't have much of a choice,' said Aadil and walked off.

The day of the first test arrived and the examination hall was full of groggy-eyed, bearded, palpitating students with fake smiles, ready to face Professor Murthy's salvo. Before the paper was distributed, the students looked at each other with sympathy, as if they were on the Titanic that had just hit the iceberg.

As expected, when the iceberg hit them, it was incisive and earth-shattering. It rattled them hard and sent them scurrying for lifeboats in a labyrinth of puzzling questions. Those who couldn't find the answers knew the icy cold waters of failure awaited them.

After a day's gap, it was time for test two. This was like Tyson's knockout punch.

On Saturday, at 8a.m. sharp, they were at Bright Future Computer Institute. They immediately got busy integrating the modules. None of them spoke much and started typing away furiously on the keyboard. Harpreet looked more pensive than usual. Barely three hours had passed when Harpreet suddenly got up and picked up his bag.

'I'm leaving. I can't do this project anymore,' he said.

Nafisa and Aadil were confused, but before they could react the door shut with a bang.

'Now what?' Nafisa asked Aadil.

Aadil had an 'I told you so' look on his face as he tried to console Nafisa.

'I don't think there's much we can do now. I knew something like this was going to happen. Looks like the strain of the tests has got to him,' said Aadil, going back to the computer.

Both of them knew that time wasn't on their side. Nafisa tried to sound optimistic and said, 'Let's work on the programmes.'

Aadil started testing the programmes and suddenly threw his arms in the air.

'Shit! There are more than 300 errors in the code. How on earth are we going to solve them? Harpreet has ditched us big time.'

Aadil looked at Nafisa and said, 'Sorry Nafisa, I don't think I can continue. I'm leaving. Let's drop this project. I don't think we can submit it by 8a.m. tomorrow.'

Without taking her eyes off the computer, a dejected Nafisa responded, 'I'll also leave in some time.'

The door creaked and shut again.

Nafisa stared blankly at the screen for some time. She could see the words 'Nafisa is a failure' written all over it.

She got up, walked up to the window and looked at the street below. The workers of Bhure Mall Sweets were arranging freshly prepared trays of sweets and snacks for the evening. Women were locked in serious negotiations with fruit and vegetable hawkers. Boys on bikes with no helmets zipped past policemen who had no inclination to stop and give them a ticket. Dishevelled holy men with bright saffron marks on their forehead walked briskly at their own pace. The world outside the window and Nafisa's mind seemed to be in disarray, searching for a purpose.

Frustrated, she went to the main office on the ground floor to drink some water.

As she poured herself some water from the cooler, she noticed a Nike plastic bag on top of it. The bag was an ordinary plastic bag but what caught Nafisa's attention were the three simple words written on it. Just do it.

She rushed to her desk and kept saying, 'Just do it, just do it.' She just felt a surge of energy engulf her. She looked at her watch and knew time wasn't on her side. She had to finish all the programmes, integrate them and do the final testing. She put her head down and worked continuously for a couple of hours. She was exhausted and went down to the street to get some fresh air.

The students of the weekend evening classes at Bright Classes had started to fill in. Thanks to Aadil's PR skills, a few students of the weekend course already knew about their software project. Nafisa followed one of the students who looked familiar.

'Hi,' said Nafisa nervously.

The nerdy boy with a goatee turned around and smiled at her, acknowledging that he remembered her.

'Hi! You are Virat. Right? How are you doing?'

'I'm good. How about you?'

'Doing well. Remember I told you about the project I was doing. Can you spare a few hours to help me complete it? I need to make the final submission tomorrow.'

Without batting an eyelid, Virat said, 'That's so cool. I'd love to help you. I have always wanted to work on a live project.'

They both went up to the computer room. After giving Virat a background of the project, Nafisa asked him to help her rectify the errors in the program. Virat had a knack for software and didn't waste too much time on picking up the logic.

Nafisa and Virat had been working for over five hours and made good progress. Nafisa looked at her watch. She then turned to Virat and said, 'Oh my god! It's nearly 7p.m. I need to get to the girl's hostel in time or there'll be a problem.'

'But then how are you going to complete the programme?'

'Yes, you are right, I'll make something up and go later.'

After a few tea and samosa breaks and more hours of backbreaking work, they were ready to test the final programme.

It was 10.30p.m. Nafisa explained the entire scenario to Virat, 'Assume a customer comes to the store and buys medicines. Check if the system updates the inventory and displays the right bill.'

Nervously, Virat entered the data one by one. He was tensed. He looked at Nafisa and saw the anxiety on her face as well. Soon Virat was ready to check the inventory screen. He closed his eyes and pressed the 'enter' key. The system took some time to display the results. Nafisa looked at the screen and matched the figures, while Virat simply kept staring at Nafisa.

'It's perfect. It's perfect. Virat, we did it. We did it!' said Nafisa, pumping the air with both fists.

Virat said with a relieved expression, 'Wow, I can't believe all the screens are working. Let me copy the programme into the floppy disk.'

Nafisa said to Virat, 'Great work, Virat. You were brilliant.'

Virat was embarrassed by her compliment and said, 'It's late. Let me drop you to your hostel road near the college.'

Nafisa sat on the pillion while Virat rode his Yamaha RX 100 through the sleepy town, through the heavily wooded roads of the university.

Sitting on the bike, experiencing a gush of cold air on her cheeks, Nafisa experienced two feelings she'd never encountered before. First was the thrill of riding behind a boy on a motorbike and second was the unadulterated joy of completing an insurmountable task. The joy of proving to the world that she could succeed when others gave-up. She'd had started to feel victorious even before participating in the contest. The bike ride with Virat felt like a victory lap in a stadium.

When they arrived at the gate of the girl's hostel, they were greeted by the enquiring eyes of the guards. When Nafisa was asked to fill out a late entry form, she knew a meeting with the hostel warden was unavoidable.

Nafisa turned to Virat and said, 'I don't know how to thank you, Virat. This wouldn't have been possible without you.'

Virat said with a boyish smile, 'Please, please, you don't have to thank me. In fact, I should be thanking you. I probably learnt more in these couple of hours than I would have in the entire course.'

'Keep in touch.'

'I definitely will. After all, I need to take a treat from you after you win the first prize,' said Virat, turning his bike and speeding away, hoping this would not be their last meeting.

He was so glad to have met her. Not only was she exceedingly bright she had a very cute, nerdy look.

***

Though most of them knew this incident well, recounting it triggered mixed feelings.

'You know Nafisa, looking back, I regret abandoning that project. Today, when I recall this incident, I think I was stupid to have walked out,' said Aadil.

'I used to wonder what made you guys quit so easily. But when I think of it now, I'm quite happy that you guys backed out. I proved that I was able to stand up to the challenge,' said Nafisa.

'Frankly speaking, I thought the entire concept was a waste of time. It lacked depth,' retorted Harpreet.

'Lacked depth? Ha ha. Dude, now your male ego is not letting you accept the fact that a woman completed something you guys left midway. In fact, today when I run my company and get bogged down by challenges, I remind myself of that project. That was my defining moment,' said Nafisa.

Harpreet's face wore a dour grimace. He had no comeback for Nafisa.

'Our egos are like our shadows. They are always with us, following us. Waiting to become bigger than us. So, we need to be careful that we don't block the light. The light of reason,' said Shivam, sounding philosophical.

'That's complicated, Shivam. Let me simplify it for you. Being egoistic is more like suffering from constipation. You feel queer and horrible from inside but try to show as if everything is normal from the outside. So, take a chill pill and junk the thoughts that cause this constipation,' added Aadil hoping to lighten the atmosphere.

'That's so true, Aadil. Our Egos can become our greatest enemies', said Nafisa agreeing with Aadil.

At this Raghav suddenly spoke up in a stern voice. 'What is this, Nafisa? We are here to spend some time together, but you've made this into some sort of therapy session. What is this rubbish? This so-called "interesting" game of yours has completely ruined the evening. I wished I'd never come here in the first place.'

Nafisa looked at Raghav with a pained expression. She was totally taken aback by his outburst. She felt terribly insulted in front of everyone.

The silence at the table was palpable.

'Guys, anyone for a smoke break?' said Francis, wanting to ease the tension.

Aadil took the hint and stood up to accompany Francis.

Raghav also got up. 'I don't smoke. But could do with some fresh air.'

Fifteen minutes later, Aadil, Francis and Raghav got back inside.

Only Aadil noticed a hint of redness in Nafisa's eyes.

Harpreet felt that he'd spoilt the mood and needed to do something immediately.

'Guys, this is an incident I'm sure all of us will remember,' said Harpreet breaking the silence.

'Hmm… All of us will remember?' asked Venky.

'Nainital 1996,' said Harpreet.

'Oh, Nainital! Now I get it,' said Venky with a knowing smile.

THE LEGEND OF DABEERA

Dalbeer Bandyopadhyay was different. He was 6 ft 3 inches tall, broad-shouldered, with a scraggly beard and curly shoulder-length hair. Born to a Bengali father and a Punjabi mother, he was like the poet, Rabindranath Tagore, who had come back to the world in a wrestler's body. Dalbeer's face mostly wore a serious expression and only two things brought a smile to it—a difficult problem and cricket. Dalbeer mostly kept to himself, but being the top scorer of the class, he was forever pestered by lesser mortals who bunked classes and then turned to Dalbeer in their hour of need. It was a foregone conclusion that Dalbeer would one day win the gold medal for being the outstanding student of the class.

The Nainital incident made the adjective 'different' for Dalbeer appear to be a gross understatement.

At the end of the second semester of the year, the college dean had a brainwave that all the four batches of the course should be sent on a recreational trip. Most of the students had no interest in this, but because it was made mandatory, they didn't have a choice. Some of the students tried to reason with the dean but to no avail.

'If you don't join the college trip, I will deduct marks for attendance,' threated the dean.

Nothing hurts students more than losing marks so the debate

ended quickly.

On the day of the departure to the Himalayan resort town of Nainital, the students could be seen jostling with each other to load their bags and rucksacks in the bus and find a place to sit with their friends. In one of the buses, the students had already started playing music but got a rude shock when they saw the dean and the other teachers board the bus.

It was a long journey and there was ample time for people to explore their hidden talents. Some tried stand-up comedy, some sang a song, some tried mimicry and some played the guitar.

Dalbeer sang the patriotic song Ekla Chalo Re. The seriousness with which he sang, coupled with his baritone, made the song amusing as well as inspiring.

Then started the ubiquitous game of a road trip, antakshari. The freshers were the most enthusiastic participants with Kunal and Preeti taking the lead from opposite teams.

Preeti first saw Kunal in the corridor when he was being ragged by the senior boys. He was made to stand there and ask every girl her hostel room number. He'd joined college that very day so to abruptly ask a girl her hostel number was a tricky situation for him. Most girls just glared at him and walked past him. Some dared him to come to the girls' hostel while others laughed him off. Preeti was rushing to the class when he asked her the same question. She lost her cool and retorted aggressively, 'Buzz off and mind your business'. That evening in the girl's hostel Kunal's ragging was the hot topic.

After that day, their interaction wasn't much but today in the bus, they hit it off well. Kunal was impressed by Preeti's singing and choice of energetic songs. After the game, Kunal went to the back seat and asked Diwakar and Manoj to move to let him sleep. An hour or so later he was woken up by a slight nudge. He lifted his hand off his eyes and saw it was Preeti.

Kunal sat down to make space for her and within no time they were chatting with each other. At one point, when Kunal was saying something to her, the bus hit a huge pothole and Kunal's head banged against Preeti's. She let out a scream.

Kunal, realizing how badly it must have hurt her, gently rubbed her head. Their eyes met and Kunal was drawn toward her and gently kissed her on the cheek. Preeti was taken aback but just for a moment, and then smiled.

In a differed part of the bus, Dalbeer changed places and sat with Harpreet. As Dalbeer rarely participated in the ragging sessions, he hardly knew anyone from the junior batch.

Surprisingly, Dalbeer and Harpreet hit it off well. They seemed to share a few things in common such as their Punjabi roots and cricket.

It was midday and almost six hours since the group had been on the road. Most of the students had dozed off except Dalbeer and Harpreet who were merrily testing each other's cricketing knowl edge.

'Okay. In the 1983 World Cup, who scored the most runs and who took the most number of wickets?' asked Dalbeer.

'That's easy. David Gower and Roger Binny,' replied Harpreet with nonchalance.

Dalbeer was impressed.

'Tell me the nickname of Vivian Richards,' asked Harpreet expecting Dalbeer to mess it up.

Dalbeer laughed and replied, 'This is what I call a sitter. Smokin' Joe. Ask some tough questions.'

'In which newspaper was the satirical obituary that started the legend of the Ashes series published?'

'The Sporting Times.'

'Off whose bowling did Sunil Gavaskar score the 10,000th run?'

'Ejaz Fakhi. That's what I call a hattrick,' said Dalbeer, with elation.

Harpreet's nonchalance soon turned to helplessness.

'Chetan Sharma took a hattrick in the 1987 world cup. Who were the batsman that got out? In the right order!'

'Ian Smith, Rutherford and Richard Hadlee,' said Dalbeer, placing an arm around Harpreet.

'Wrong,' said Harpreet, looking blankly at Dalbeer.

'Wrong? What do you mean wrong?'

'The third batsman was Ewen Chatfield.'

'What rubbish! The right answer is Richard Hadlee,' protested Dalbeer.

Dalbeer was so loud that a couple of students woke up startled.

But Harpreet was not going be cowered down by Dalbeer's rant. He simply pulled out an edition of 'The Cricket quiz book' from his bag and threw it on Dalbeer's lap. Dalbeer was tempted to read the book up to be sure, but he didn't want to be further embarrassed and so he returned the book without checking the answer.

The two sat silently, like a married couple that had had a spat, for the remainder of the bus trip.

The group reached Nainital. Everyone was booked into a room with two students each. To keep things simple, those who travelled together were given the same room. Much to their consternation, Dalbeer and Harpreet found themselves in the same room on the fourth floor of the Lake View hotel in Nainital.

The long journey over the hilly terrain had fatigued the group but after they took one look at the scenic landscape, they were itching to get out and explore Nainital.

The next morning, the group trekked up to China Peak, from where the mountains on the Tibetan border could be seen. It was an arduous climb but the mesmerising beauty from the peak was so invigorating that everyone forgot the hardships on the way.

After a day of trekking on the hills, a night bonfire was organized. Harpreet enjoyed himself by the fire but soon felt drowsy.

He walked up to his room thinking that Dalbeer would have slept by then but hopefully not locked the door. He turned the doorknob and was surprised to find the door locked. He knocked on the door. There was no reply. He knocked again. No reply. Harpreet got irritated and banged on the door.

Harpreet was losing patience. He was thinking of what to do next when there was a loud thud on the door. It appeared as though something had hit the door from inside with brute force. The sound shattered the silence of the night.

Harpreet wondered why Dalbeer was trying to hit the door when it was locked from inside. Just then, the door opened and he saw Dalbeer's tall and well-built frame standing in the doorway.

Harpreet looked at Dalbeer and shouted on his face, 'Are you mad? Why the hell did you close the door?'

Harpreet was about to enter the room to sleep when he noticed something peculiar about Dalbeer. From the light of the corridor that fell on Dalbeer's face, he noticed his eyes were shut. Eyes shut, breathing heavily, Dalbeer stood there mumbling to himself.

Dalbeer was sleepwalking.

Instinctively, Harpreet turned around to run. But in a flash, Dalbeer's long arms reached out and pushed him against the wall. Harpreet felt Dalbeer's wrist hit him on his neck. For a moment, he seemed to lose his breath. But he quickly recovered himself and started running towards the staircase. Dalbeer seemed to be possessed and darted after him as he chased Harpreet.

Instead of turning right for the stairs, Harpreet turned left into the toilets. He quickly ran and shut the door of one of the cubicles. But before he could bolt it, Dalbeer's heavy hand pushed it open. Harpreet jumped back and quickly placed his feet on the commode seat and looked at Dalbeer, waiting for him to make the next move. Surprisingly, his eyes were still wide shut and he was still breathing heavily.

Harpreet turned and jumped on the commode, put his hands on the partition between the cubicles and lifted himself. Lying on the dusty partition between the toilet cubicles, he looked at Dalbeer down below, heaving a sigh of relief.

Dalbeer stood there for a few seconds and then left.

Shashank was a lighter sleeper and was woken up by the commotion. He had barely stepped out and closed his door when he saw a strange sight. A person wearing pyjamas and an open shirt was sitting on a chair, a few feet away from his room. The person sat upright with his hands one on top of the other as if he was guarding his room.

Shashank recognized Dalbeer and started to walk towards him.

'Hey Dalbeer, what are you doing?'

Shashank could not make out that Dalbeer's eyes were closed.

Just then, Dalbeer suddenly got up, stood for a couple of seconds and threw his chair at Shashank. The back of the chair hit Shashank's foot. But instead of bothering to see how badly he was hit, Shashank quickly turned and bolted towards the staircase like a rabbit. Dalbeer was after him like a greyhound.

Shashank was short and nimble and was able to rush down the staircase. Dalbeer clambered down but couldn't catch Shashank.

Shashank was out of breath when he reached the ground floor and ran to the receptionist. He thanked his stars that Dalbeer had given up the chase.

'Call our dean. Quickly. Quickly. One of our students has gone crazy. He threw a chair at me.'

'Okay, I'll do that. But who is he and why,' asked the receptionist in his usual trained-to-be-calm voice.

'Please first call somebody quickly,' blurted Shashank.

Harpreet reached the ground floor and was surprised to see Shashank.

'Dude, what's happened to Dalbeer? He seems to have lost his mind,' said Shashank deliriously. His voice was mixed with fear and panic.

'I don't know. I think he's sleepwalking. I'm not going to stay in the same room as him.'

'But where is he now?'

'He chased me then he disappeared. Let's hear what the dean has to say.'

The dean and other professors reached the reception. In the next ten minutes, the reception was full of students and a few curious onlookers.

The dean walked up to Harpreet and Shashank.

'Where is Dalbeer?'

'We don't know sir. He chased Shashank and me on the fourth floor. But disappeared after that. We've no clue where he went.'

'This is serious. Not only is he a threat to the people around him but also to himself. Let us split ourselves into batches of three each and search the floors and see if we can find him,' ordered Dean Adhikari.

This situation brought out a very different avatar of the dean. Like a seasoned policeman, he marshalled his pyjama clad troops for the comb and search operation. Two members of the hotel staff also joined the operations. Each batch was assigned a floor. Some were cursing themselves for coming out of their rooms while the others saw this as an adventure.

After an hour, all the groups were back in the reception with no trace of Dalbeer.

This time the dean had an extremely perplexed expression on his face.

'If we are not able to find him, we'll have to report the case to the police. He may have walked out of the hotel complex.'

Everyone was fatigued and needed rest. So, the dean ordered tea for everyone. People started sipping tea and gossiping nonstop when the dean asked to meet the duty manager.

The dean got up and asked the duty manager, 'We've looked in a lot of places but I'm sure we've left out a few places. Where do you suggest we look?'

The duty manager called one of the staff members for a side conversation. The duty manager then asked the group.

'Have you checked the terrace?'

The faces wore a blank expression.

'Don't you lock the terrace every night?' asked the dean.

'Yes we do, but last night we had some labourers working. So, the contractor has the key. It's possible that they may have left it open.'

The dean immediately gestured to everyone to leave their tea cups and rush to the terrace. The open door of the roof could mean a lot of things.

As suspected the door was ajar. The dean's eyes narrowed. He looked worried, not sure what he would find.

The group slowly eased into the terrace with their torches. The cold night air hit the group and instantly drove away their sleep. At one glance, one could make out that there was no one around, apart from some equipment left behind by the labourers.

Shashank and Harpreet broke away from the others and started looking around more seriously.

Harpreet stopped Shashank and pointed at a distance. Behind a corner of the terrace, something fluttered in the wind.

They walked towards the wall and saw it was Dalbeer's hair fluttering. He was sitting on the ground and sleeping.

Shashank immediately waved to the others and motioned them to be quiet.

Harpreet bent down to see if his eyes were closed. Sure enough, they were tightly shut.

The group got closer and decided that he should be carried down.

Four able bodied boys lifted him carefully, making sure that he didn't wake up. When they had just begun carrying him, they heard a sound, as if something had fallen from his body. The dean pointed his torch to see what it was. Harpreet nudged Shashank to give way so that he could get a better look at what had fallen.

In the light of the torch, Harpeet saw something familiar.

It was his Cricket Quiz book.

***

'The shocking bit was Dalbeer had no memory of the incident,' said Harpreet.

'When he met us for breakfast the next morning, he sat next to me as if nothing had happened. In fact, he complimented me on my cricket knowledge.'

'That day two athletes were born—one a high jumper and other a sprinter but sadly they never went onto represent India,' said Francis jokingly.

'Harpreet hope you've now stopped testing people's general knowledge,' said Nafisa also chipping in.

'C'mon Nafisa, you've no idea how crazy that night was. But back in the day, running fast wasn't my only talent. There were others.

I'll tell you guys in a bit. But let's order some more beers first', said Harpreet.

Harpreet called the waiter and asked for the drink's menu. For the next ten minutes, Harpreet and Francis spent deciding which beer to order. After getting thoroughly confused by the plethora of options, they repeated the same order.

'Folks now is the time for incident when we proved to the world that you can't mess with geeks', said Harpreet excitedly.

'Yes, I remember that the time when we'd just become seniors and wanted to boss around our juniors', said Shivam

'I wish Prabhat was here. He would have loved telling this story. But let me do the honours nonetheless', said Harpreet

SCREW ROXY

By the end of first semester Prabhat had acquired the reputation of being the batch toughie. He'd created a small gang that wouldn't hesitate to pick up a fight with just about anybody. The second semester results were just out and he was the happiest of the batch. Not because he managed to scrape through the exams but because he would now become a senior and would get to rag the juniors.

The junior batch had started to get their hostel rooms allocated in the same building as the seniors. This was deliberately done so that the batch could intermingle.

Prabhat defined the rules of ragging. Before dinner all juniors had to assemble in his room where he would be with his gang ready to pounce on one of them and rag him till late in the night.

One night, the batch of juniors were lined-up in his room as he did a crude imitation of the villain Gabbar Singh from the film *Sholay*.

'How many girls were there?' said Prabhat trying to sound like Gabbar.

No one uttered a word.

'Didn't you hear. I asked you, how many girls were there?'

Still no response.

Prabhat now in an even sterner voice, 'Nobody wants to tell us how many girls are in your batch, eh?'

Then a solitary voice spoke up.

'Six'

Prabhat was pleased to hear an answer. He looked at the fresher. It was Shekhar who had joined the same day.

Prabhat walked up to him.

'So, who do you think is the best looking?'

'None,' said Shekhar with a straight face.

'Oh, really, pretty boy? You think you are some stud that you didn't find anyone worthy?' said Prabhat moving his hand towards Shekhar's face as if to pat his cheek.

But before Prabhat's right hand could touch Shekhar's face, he caught Prabhat's hand. Prabhat's left hand whipped out, slapping Shekhar hard on the face. Shekhar was not going to let Prabhat get away with this, so he pushed Prabhat so hard that he fell down on the ground.

Prabhat was stunned. He swiftly got up to attack Shekhar but his batchmates held him back.

'Let go of me. I want to teach this bastard a lesson', shouted a struggling Prabhat. But the others held him tight.

Seeing the tension escalate, Rohit thought it best to abandon the ragging for the night and he asked everyone to leave.

***

One Friday evening Prabhat, Rohit, Vinay and a couple of others were at the market sipping juices and ogling at the girls from the hostel.

'Hey, Rohit, why don't you walk up to the girl in blue jeans there and propose to her', said Prabhat pointing towards the group standing in the market.

'Why don't go yourself, if you think you are such a dude?' replied Rohit.

'Of course, I can go. I'm not scared', said Prabhat wiping the juice off his lips.

Rahul was about to walk towards the crowd he saw a group of men approaching them. From the distance, he noticed a familiar face. As they got closer, Prabhat recognized Shekhar from the junior batch.

'He's the one', said Shekhar to a man pointing to Prabhat.

The man walked up to Prabhat.

'So, you are one the ragging the juniors, eh?'

Prabhat just stared at the man. He was of average height and of lean built.

'Shekhar is my cousin and I dare any of you to touch him again.'

'We'll see about that', said Prabhat with a snigger.

In an instant, Shekhar's brother lashed out at Prabhat and slapped him as hard as he could.

Prabhat was too stunned to react. He couldn't imagine someone having the guts to pick up a fight in a crowded market.

Rohit and Vinay jumped from their seats to retaliate but a solid push from one of the guys was enough for them to back-off.

Prabhat and his friends beat a hasty retreat from the market but couldn't digest this embarrassment.

Shekhar's insolence had gone too far. The following week kept them busy with exams but every night of that week they discussed plans on how get even with him.

***

'I've found out what Shekhar's cousin does,' shouted Rohit as he barged into Prabhat's room.

'Okay, good! Where can we find him?' asked Prabhat excitedly.

'He runs a small computer training school a few kilometres away from the University', said Rohit.

Shiva, who was also in Prabhat's room spoke. 'It's pathetic that it's been so many days and we've not done anything to these buggers. Time to teach them a lesson.'

Hearing this from Shiva gave everyone a lot of confidence. They all nodded their heads.

'You guys finish tomorrow's exam and then let's sort these cousins out', said Shiva shaking Prabhat's hand and walking out of the room.

The next afternoon after they finished their exam, they decided to execute their plan. Like typical gangsters from the movies they rode on their bikes and scooters towards the market. They were all pumped up. Vinay was a little tense but upon seeing Prabhat and Shiva's confidence, he too acted cool.

They reached the market and parked their vehicles a distance from Roxy Computers. From a distance they identified, Rajbir, Shekhar's cousin who'd slapped Prabhat in the market. He was talking to someone outside his shop.

They all walked up to him and before he could react, pushed him hard.

'Who do you think you are? You can come into the college just like that and hit one of us?' said Shiva

Rajbir's head hit the glass pane of the training centre. He was stunned for a moment but still defiant. The others rallied around Shiva and surrounded Rajbir.

Suddenly, the door of Roxy Computers opened. There stood in a frame a sight they hadn't expected at all. Shekhar's man-mountain second brother, Gajendra, looked menacingly at them.

Prabhat and the boys saw fear in Shiva's eyes for the first time. He began to retreat slowly. Gajendra noticed him trying to run, so swiftly in one leap, he got hold of Prabhat and gave him a solid punch on his shoulder. Prabhat tried to be brave and rushed to push Gajendra. But it turned out to be a big mistake.

Gajendra shoved him aside and wrapped his arms around Prabhat who struggled like a baby. Gajendra swung him around and pushed him onto the ground. All this happened so fast that the others simply had no time to react. Vinay did what he knew best—run back to the scooter. Shiva stood frozen like a statue of the Hindu God with the same name as him.

Their plan had turned out to be a fiasco. Shiva, Prabhat and the others high-tailed as the onlookers in the market laughed at them. Gajendra and Rajbir went back into the training centre as if nothing had happened.

News of this incident spread faster than wildfire and soon they were the butt of jokes in the hostel. Every hosteler's favourite in-between studies topic was 'How Prabhat got screwed'. Prabhat's reputation was reduced from the batch toughie to that of the batch loser. Shekhar, Rajbir and Gajendra had proven that he was nothing but a paper tiger. Even the girls found out about this incident. They tried to be sympathetic towards him but behind his back they would have a good laugh.

One evening, Prabhat and the gang were having dinner together and Harpreet was sitting next to him. Harpreet looked at Prabhat and the gang and remarked. 'You guys really let us engineers down. You went to bash these city fellows but got thrashed instead.'

'Oh yeah? If you'd tried to take on that hulk, he would have skewered you in the dhaba next to his training centre,', replied Prabhat.

'Guys, sorry to say, but you didn't play to your strengths.'

'What do you mean we didn't play to our strengths?' asked Prabhat sarcastically.

'Meet me tomorrow at the computer class and I'll explain,' said Harpreet.

Next day at the computer class, after the lab teacher had given everyone an assignment and left, Harpreet called Prabhat and the others.

'Let me show you something', said Harpreet with a mischievous smile.

Harpreet loaded a disk and pressed a few keys. They all looked at the screen that popped up.

'Okay guys now press a button,' continued Harpreet.

Prabhat pressed a key. But nothing happened. He pressed again. The result was the same. Rohit pitched in and rapidly hit a few keys.

'You idiot, nothing is happening. What the hell is this?'

'You fool. Next time you go home, ask your mother to pack you some *badams* for your brains. This is a freaking computer virus,' said Harpreet arrogantly.

'I developed this virus. Once installed on one computer, it copies itself through the network and screws all computers. It can only be removed by formatting the computer. I hope I don't need to explain what you need to do next,' continued Harpreet.

'Give me this virus, we'll get someone who attends classes at Roxy Computers to install it on one of his personal computers', said Prabhat with a vengeful look on his face. This plan gave him hope of restoring his tattered reputation.

'Guys, to make your revenge even sweeter, here's what I'll put on the screen', said Harpeet with a twinkle in his eyes. He quickly made some changes and the screen flashed a fist with a middle finger sticking out.

'This is cool Harpreet,' said Prabhat, giving him a high five.

***

Over the next few days, Prabhat and the gang scouted around the hostel for someone who could help execute their plans. They found out that one of the juniors, Ashish, attended classes at the coaching institute and they coerced him into joining the team to carry out operation Screw Roxy.

A week later, when there were a lot of students at the institute and Gajendra and Ashish were busy managing them, Ashish quietly copied the programme onto one of the machines and left.

Late in the evening, from a distance, Prabhat and the gang watched Gajendra and Rajbir lock-up for the day. They waited for the market to shut down completely. Once they were sure nobody was watching, Rohit and Vinay picked up the ladder with had brought with them and ran towards Roxy. Prabhat followed them with posters and a can of industrial glue.

'Rohit, put the ladder slowly against the centre's signboard,' said Vinay.

Vinay and Rohit held the ladder while Prabhat walked up carefully to the top. Vinay passed Prabhat posters with glue on one side. Balancing himself on the ladder he softly pasted the two posters on the signboard. Mission accomplished, they quickly got back to the hostel.

***

Next morning, Gajendra rode into the market on his Enfield 500 and parked it outside the road. He was walking towards the centre when his eye caught something unusual on the signboard. He was shocked when he read it. Sexy Computers instead of Roxy Computers.

'Who is the bastard who's done this?' swore Gajendra as he opened the lock. He was fuming.

He immediately called his brother. 'Rajbir, those morons from the University have defaced our sign-board. Come here quickly with a ladder.' Rajbir got the message and left immediately for the market.

Meanwhile, Gajendra looked at the watch and realized it was time for the morning batch of students to come in. He switched on the master switch to fire-up all the computers at the centre.

Within a couple of minutes, the systems started but instead of the Windows logo, all he could see were hands showing him the middle finger.

Gajendra froze. He knew he was screwed.

***

'So, guys what happened after that. Didn't they come after you', asked Nafisa

'They did. In fact, they came into the hostel and created a huge ruckus. But those guys also realized they couldn't mess with us. In fact, some months later Gajendra met me and requested me for some help,' replied Harpreet.

'What help did he want?' asked Nafisa

'Fixing computer viruses,' said Harpreet with a chuckle.

Just then, the waiter returned.

'Everything fine here? Can I get you guys something?'

Shivam jumped at the opportunity. 'Ah yes. Let's repeat the snacks and also the drinks.'

Everybody looked at Shivam, amazed at his love for food.

'Okay everyone, if nobody's starting, I'm next,' declared Shivam.

The others were more than happy to let Shivam start his story.

ONLY TEN MINUTES

Professor Prasad turned away from the blackboard and scanned the classroom like a T-90 tank's turret searching for its victim. Sitting in the middle of the classroom, Shivam Bhatti could sense his palpitations start and felt his throat go dry. He looked down and said a silent prayer. He hoped he was not the chosen one.

'Shivam Bhatti,' said Prof. Prasad gently.

'Could you be so kind to enlighten this uninformed class on the implications of a direct current of 5 ampere on the components of this trivial circuit?'

The T-90 shell had nailed its target. Shivam was impacted less by the TNT in the shell but more by the chaste English that wrapped it.

Reeling under the daze of the impact, Shivam got up to answer the question. He looked at the circuit and blurted out.

'Sir, the capacitor will brusht with this current.'

Barely had he finished when the whole class started laughing.

'Burst not brusht,' said Prof. Prasad correcting Shivam's faux pas.

The incident left an indelible mark on Shivam's psyche. Whenever he spoke in class, he could picture his classmates ready to laugh at his poor English.

A month or so after the incident, when Shivam was walking out of a class, he noticed a bright poster on the notice board. It read, 'Invitation for paper presentations at Tech-O-Mania, the annual technical festival of VH Technological Institute, Mumbai.' Shivam glanced at it and quickly passed his classmates who were intently reading it, especially Aditya Mukherji. Aditya was an exceptional speaker and rarely came back to college without a prize.

After dinner, Shivam decided to take a walk all by himself.

Shivam took his usual route up to the college gate and was headed back to the hostel. As he was nearing the lane for the academic block, he suddenly got an idea. He quickly turned towards the academic block.

He was peering through the window of the main gate when he heard the tapping of a wooden stick against the ground.

'Do you intend to break down the door?' asked the college guard with a strong Haryanvi accent.

Shivam turned around quickly.

'I've forgotten my notes in the class,' said Shivam.

'Okay then take them tomorrow morning,' said the guard.

'I have a test in the morning.'

'We are not allowed to open the class once it's closed. You'll have to come in the morning.'

'Please, I request you.'

'Get a faculty's permission.'

'Please it's a sincere request.'

'No.'

'Please, it's a sincere and humble request.'

'Okay, but make it quick,' said the guard in an annoyed voice.

The guard opened the door and switched on the lights. Then he followed Shivam to his classroom upstairs.

Shivam entered his classroom and searched furiously. Then he announced.

'I think someone's taken it.'

'Okay then let's go.'

'Wait a minute. Do you have a pen and paper?'

'Yes. Why do you need it?'

Shivam didn't wait to answer. He quickly ran to the notice board and scribbled the topic of the contest and rushed back.

The guard gave him an irritated glance and locked the door.

Over the next two weeks, Shivam rushed to the library after class hours to collect material for his paper.

Finally, a day before the submission, he was satisfied to see his thirty-page paper and a slide presentation on 'Application of robotics for wheelchair mobility over stairs.'

A month later, during a break between classes, the office attendant entered the class. He looked around and asked, 'Who's Shivam Bhatti? There's a package for him.'

Shivam was busy making notes and was surprised by this announcement. He collected the package and was preparing to put it in his bag.

Sahil took it from Shivam's hand and read it aloud.

'VH Technological Institute. Technical paper presentation.'

Aditya Mukherji, who was talking to a bunch of friends, heard this and walked up to Shivam.

He looked at the package, sniggered and left the class room.

Shivam reached his room and opened the package quickly and read through the letter hurriedly. As he read the word 'selected', he pumped his fist in the air and let out a loud 'yes'.

His excitement slowly turned into apprehension as he pictured himself mumbling in front of a confused audience. The paper presentation was in just two weeks and he had to get ready for it immediately.

Every day, after dinner, Shivam walked around the campus recalling sections of his paper and reciting them loudly. On one occasion, he recited it so loudly that a cyclist turned around and gave him a sympathetic look. The cyclist probably thought that the pressure of studies had got to him.

Shivam reached Mumbai by train on the day of the presentation.

Shivam gorged on the lunch that the organizers had arranged for everyone. He was about to finish when he heard the announcement for the paper presenters. He quickly finished his food and reached the hall where all the students from colleges across the country had gathered.

There was a help desk where students could check their names for the presentation. Shivam got to the desk and peered through sheets looking for his name. At the first glance, he didn't find it. He looked through it again and the result was the same.

A nonplussed Shivam spoke to the volunteers at the help desk. 'My name's not there.'

The student at the table replied, 'Let me check.' She looked at the sheet and then at the confirmation letter. Giving Shivam a surprised yet concerned look , she said, 'There seems to be a mistake, let me check with the faculty.'

The girl walked up to a group of teachers having their lunch. She turned to Assistant Professor Vikas Dhawan and requested him to spare a moment.

The student and Professor Dhawan spoke for about fifteen minutes, after which the girl came back and said to Shivam, 'You were supposed to confirm your presence for the event. Our letter to you mentions this. We didn't receive any confirmation from your side, so the slot was given to someone else.'

Shivam stood there looking confused. He stared blankly at the girl as she returned his confirmation letter to him. He took the letter and walked out of the hall. He reached the courtyard, wondering what he should do next.

Shivam was too embarrassed. He had made an overnight train journey to be told that he couldn't present his paper at the contest. With a heavy heart, he walked out of the campus gate. He kept walking till he reached the main road. The sun was strong, but it didn't matter to Shivam. Across the road, he saw a ramshackle tea stall. He went to the tea stall and sat down on one of the benches outside. The stall seemed to be a favourite haunt of truck drivers and a few students who seemed to have all the time in the world.

Shivam asked the tea stall owner, 'A cup of tea. And do you know what time the next train to Kanpur is?'

The tea stall owner replied, 'There's one in two hours and then one early morning.'

Shivam sat down on the bench and pulled out the confirmation letter and began to read through it.

Dear Mr. Bhatti,

This is to inform you that your paper has been selected for the presentation. We look forward to hosting you in our campus for the presentation…

Shivam read through the letter a couple times, but he found no mention of an acknowledgment as a prerequisite for presenting the paper. He quickly gulped down the tea, paid for the tea and walked back to the campus.

Shivam walked back to the hall and looked for the girl whom he had spoken to earlier.

'Excuse me, can I speak to you for a moment?'

The girl replied, 'Yeah sure, tell me.'

'I went through the letter and I didn't find any mention of the acknowledgment in the letter,' said Shivam.

The girl was confused, 'Hmm, it must be there. Let me see it.' She took the letter and glanced through it quickly. 'Looks like you got the previous version. I'm pretty sure we had put it in the updated letter.'

'This is the letter I got. If it's not there, how I am supposed to know that an acknowledgment is required? Can you please make an exception and give me a slot?'

The girl was insistent, 'No, this is not possible. We've not had any dropouts. I'm sorry I can't do anything.'

Shivam started to walk away from there even before she completed her sentence. On the way, he saw Assistant Professor Dhawan, who was the convener of the paper presentation. Professor Dhawan looked so young that people mostly mistook him for a student.

Shivam pleaded with him. 'I've come all the way to give the presentation. Please consider my case and give me a slot.'

Professor Dhawan was adamant, 'All the slots are taken. I can't do anything now.'

Just then, a good-looking female student walked up to Professor Dhawan and said, 'Sir, can I discuss the paper with you?' Professor Dhawan glared at her and said, 'Not now.' But the girl persisted and insisted on speaking to him for a few minutes. The professor looked at her very sternly and she got the message.

Shivam was dejected. He knew it was all over for him.

On his way out of the campus, Shivam's again caught sight of Professor Dhawan and the good-looking female student. They were standing in a secluded corner and talking. The girl seemed quite animated and kept trying to hold the professor's hand. The professor seemed to be giving her a reassuring look. They finished their conversation and the girl walked away. The manner in which the two of them had interacted didn't seem right to Shivam.

He walked back to the registration desk where students from other institutes were present. He walked up to one of them and introduced himself. He then said, 'Did you send an acknowledgment letter after you got your confirmation letter?' The student said, 'No, I don't think we had to.'

When he heard this, Shivam was frustrated. He stormed out of the hall angrily. He pulled out a paper and pen and began to write a letter to the dean. He rewrote the letter three times before he was satisfied.

To

The Dean
VH Technological Institute

Dear Sir/Madam,

Despite my paper being accepted by your institute, I have been unfairly excluded from presenting my paper. I have travelled all the way to your institute, but I have been asked to return as I haven't given an acknowledgment letter. There seems to be some misunderstanding by the organizing committee and I would appreciate if you could let me present the paper.

Look forward to hearing from you.

Sincerely,
Shivam Bhatti
3rd year student,
Mathewson Institute of Technology

Shivam walked up to the peon sitting outside the dean's office and said to him, 'I need to speak to the dean and give him this letter.'

The peon took the letter but replied with disinterest, 'He's not here at the moment but I'll give this to him once he's back.'

Shivam had no choice but to leave the letter with the peon of the dean and leave the campus.

A day ago, he had been on the same train travelling with excitement about the paper he was going to present. But today, he was back on the same train feeling embarrassed and dejected. He also had a lot of questions. Was Prof. Dhawan actually an upright person or was there was something fishy going on between him and the female student?

Shivam reached his institute and went straight to his hostel room. He was too embarrassed to meet anyone. The next morning, he couldn't concentrate on the lectures. It was also very difficult for him to explain to his batchmates what had happened. Some were sympathetic with him, but most of them couldn't care less.

After classes, Shivam walked towards his hostel. Suddenly, one of his hostel mates approached him and said, 'Shivam, there's a call for you.'

Shivam wondered who it was. With trepidation, he went to the hostel common room to take the call.

'Hello, Shivam speaking.'

There was an authoritative voice at the other end.

'Shivam, this is the dean of VH Technological Institute. I understand that you had been selected to present a paper at our institute. However, due to a mix-up on our part, we couldn't accommodate you during your allocated segment. Since the festival is still on, we would like to present your paper on the last day. We would appreciate it if you can come to our institute by day after tomorrow afternoon to present your paper. I know it's an inconvenience to make such a long trip again, but we would be happy to reimburse your travel expense. So Shivam, would we have the pleasure of meeting you?'

There was a long silence after this. Shivam was too astounded to say anything at first. He then quickly blurted out, 'Yes sir, yes sir, certainly.'

After the call, Shivam quickly packed his bags and rushed to the railway station. He managed to find a seat on a train that would drop him at VH Technological Institute on time.

Shivam was excited to be back in the campus and all pumped up to present the paper.

As he approached the main gate of the institute, he saw an open jeep. One of the boys looked at him and got off it swiftly.

'Oh, so you are the guy who complained about Prof Dhawan?' said the boy in a threatening tone.

Shivam ignored him and started to walk past.

Before Shivam could react, the boy turned around, put his fore-arm around his neck and squeezed it hard.

Just then, two other boys got off the jeep and rushed towards Shivam. One of them caught Shivam's legs and took him behind the jeep. They threw him on the ground and started kicking him on his body.

'You bastard, you want to present a paper in the contest. First, present that paper to us!' said one of the boys.

'You will not present the paper. Go back to the railway station or you'll be in no state to even get home,' said another.

The boys gave him one hard kick and Shivam rolled close to the rear tires of the jeep. Shivam just lay under the shade of the jeep. Ten minutes later, he sat up with great difficulty. His whole body was sore. He could feel his nose was moist with blood. With great difficulty he got up on his feet, dusted his clothes and hair and started walking.

He was relieved to see his shoulder bag where the first boy had caught him. As he picked it up, he noticed that the boys were still loitering outside the gate, daring him to enter the building.

The boys thought that beating up Shivam would scare him, but they didn't factor the irrationality that pervades human behaviour. In spite of a ninety-nine per cent chance of being thrashed again, Shivam walked defiantly towards the college gate instead of the bus stop. One of the boys who had kicked Shivam started approaching him. Shivam saw his clenched fists and knew a punch was coming his way. Shivam's heart began to pound fast.

In his nervousness, Shivam stared back at him and blurted, 'I will present the paper. Do whatever you want.'

The boy was now seething with anger and was about to punch Shivam when his friends, seeing a crowd around them, stopped him. They backed off and let Shivam walk to the main building.

Shivam looked at his watch. He still had forty-five minutes to go before his talk. He quickly walked to the canteen and asked for some water. He took the bottle and gulped it hurriedly.

The auditorium was full of students, professors and contestants from across the country. It was the last day of the technical festival and Shivam was given the last slot in the evening.

In the front were the chief guest of the event, the dean, heads of departments and Professor Dhawan. Professor Dhawan was shocked to see him in the room. One of the judges looked at Shivam and said, 'Please start, you have only ten minutes.'

'Thank you for giving me an opportunity to present my paper in front of this esteemed audience. As you may be aware, it is not easy being physically challenged anywhere in the world, but it is more difficult in India, where hardly any attention is paid to make mobility easy for the differently abled.'

After this brief introduction, Shivam illustrated his design of a wheelchair that would allow physically challenged people to climb stairs. Everybody listened in rapt attention to this interesting concept.

'Thank you very much, I still have two minutes for questions.'

Shivam stepped down from the podium, and saw the dean nodding his head in approval.

Shivam Bhatti had found his voice.

***

'Shivam, I didn't know you went through all this,' said Aadil.

'It's commendable that despite being beaten up, you wanted to give the talk,' said Raghav.

'I was more scared of facing you guys when I landed at the hostel without giving the talk. Guys, but honestly today when I look back to that day, I think it completely transformed me. Not only did I lose my fear of public speaking but as you know a few years later I proposed to the girl from VH College. The girl at the help-desk who'd assisted me, joined the same post graduate course and today she's my wife,' said Shivam with an impish smile.

Everyone clapped for Shivam, except Francis. 'But dude what had really happened. Why didn't they give you a slot in the first place? Did you ever find out?', asked Francis

'Remember I told you about the girl who was getting very cosy with the Professor. They were both having an affair. She was the one who wanted to present a paper but by the time she applied there were no speaker slots left. She convinced the Professor to drop a name and replace it with hers. And that name coincidentally happened to be mine,' explained Shivam.

Venky also clapped with the others but seemed to be lost in his own world. He recalled an incident that was buried but not dead in his graveyard of forgotten episodes. Venkat thought it was time he let the skeleton out and kill it forever.

EUREKA

Venky got out of the university railway station and searched for an autorickshaw. He'd barely walked fifty paces when he noticed an autorickshaw parked next to the closed shops.

'Mathewson?' asked Venky, peering into the darkness of the autorickshaw.

The driver woke up slowly from the passenger seat and nodded his head. Venky got into the back and waited for the driver to start the autorickshaw. Venky looked at his watch. It was nearly 1a.m. Venky had just returned from Chennai where he had participated in a cultural event.

Though he had won the second prize in the singing competition, it was little consolation to him. He was very nervous about the electronics practical exam that very morning. He cursed himself for spending too much time with the girls of the organizing committee over coffee and vadas because of which he had to take the late-night train. To make matters worse, he hardly got any sleep on the way, thanks to his co-passengers who were practicing wedding songs on the way to a marriage function.

Venky woke up with a jolt when the autorickshaw driver stopped in front of the hostel gate.

'Forty rupees,' said the driver.

Venky looked at the driver's eyes as he paid him. They were alert. He envied him.

Venky walked into the hostel gate and saw a room with a light on. He quickly dropped his stuff in his room and quickly went to see what was going on.

He reached the room and gave the door a solid kick. The door flung open and he saw huddled in one room, fifteen of his batch-mates. Seven on the bed, four on the writing table and two leaning on the bookshelf. Two were seated on a chair each. The only place unoccupied was the ceiling fan.

Raghav looked at Venky with concern and said, 'Dude, Professor Murthy has screwed us. In tomorrow's practical exam, we will have to make the circuits diagrams ourselves from scratch. It's not an open book exam.'

'What! This is crap. He clearly said we don't need to remember any circuits. All we need to do is to assemble them and see the output. I'm totally screwed, man,' exclaimed Venky, hitting his palm on his forehead.

'Well, all of us are screwed. We also got to know very late. There are thirty-five circuit diagrams and he can pick any.'

Venky was too tired to think of anything. He picked up his bag and went to his room. He sat on the table, opened the book and flipped to the first page of the chapter. 'Digital Circuits: An Introduction.' His eyes began to shut and he gave in and put his head down.

***

The silence in Venky's room was interrupted by the sound of a light thud. It was his wake-up alarm. Venky had instructed the newspaper boy to throw the newspaper through the ventilator so that it landed straight on his bed.

Venky lifted his head from the study table and looked at the book again. The words 'Digital Circuits: An Introduction' stared backed at him. He jumped with a sudden jolt.

'Oh hell!' screamed Venky. He had slept through the night without turning even a page. He looked at the watch. It was 6.30a.m. Nothing much could be done now. He walked towards the washroom only to be interrupted by Ashish in the hallway.

'How is it going, dude? Heard you got the second prize in singing.'

'Yeah man. It was good. How is your prep for the practicals?'

'I have done like twenty-five circuits. I will take a chance on the rest.'

'Okay buddy, got to rush,' said Venky with pronounced nervousness.

Even in the washroom, all he could hear was discussions about the exam. He quickly finished brushing and started walking back to his room. He was walking quickly when he glanced at one of the rooms. The door was half open and Devender was at his desk writing. He walked up to him and looked at what Devender was doing.

Devender was carefully drawing circuit diagrams. Venky looked closely. They were small sheets of paper.

'What are these?' asked Venky.

'Don't you know what these are? You moron—cheat sheets!'

'I've never used them,' said Venky with pride.

'Okay, great. Now buzz off.'

Venky was taking a shower and thinking hard about how to get out of the mess. When all of a sudden, an idea struck him. Like Archimedes, he jumped out of the bathroom and ran to Devender's room.

'Give me some of your sheets,' Venky said to Devender.

Devender couldn't control his laughter when he saw Venky standing in front of him with only a towel round his waist; wet dishevelled hair and water dripping on the floor.

'Ha ha! What happened now, Mr I-Don't-Use-Cheat-Sheets? Copy them quickly and return them to me,' said Devender, with a snigger.

Venky returned to his room looking at the sheets. They were small pieces of paper with circuits intricately etched on them. Devender's handwriting was excellent and they looked like prints.

He quickly got dressed and rushed to the college photocopier's shop. Venky asked the shopkeeper to print copies of the cheat sheets.

The boy spread the cheat sheets on the photocopier and out came the copies. Venky carefully cut each of the diagrams into small chits. He walked back to Devender's room and returned the sheets to him.

'You wrote them pretty fast, eh,' remarked a surprised Devender.

'No dude. I just used some brains. See these.'

Devender saw his handwritten sheets in black photocopied ink. 'This is crazy! You even copied the sheet for copying,' said Devender.

Just then, Saahil entered Devender's room to return his shaving cream. 'What's going on, guys?'

Saahil saw the small chits in Venky's hands. 'What the hell are these? You bugger! You photocopied the diagrams. Gosh, you will get caught,' warned Saahil and stormed out of the room.

Devender and Venky looked at each other with the chits in their hand.

Suddenly, the door opened and Saahil was there again. 'Do you have the chit for the amplifier circuit? That one's is a bit complicated.'

Within the next thirty minutes, half the batch of the class had lined up outside the photocopier's shop. Most of them copied at least one circuit diagram that they were most scared of.

Soon the examination hall slowly filled in with nervous students. The question papers were distributed.

To everyone's shock, Prof. Murthy threw another surprise at them. The circuit diagrams were given and they only had to assemble them.

Professor Verma was invigilating the practical exam. The atmosphere was quite relaxed.

Venky looked at the question paper. It was now very easy with the diagrams given. Soon he was completely engrossed in assembling the components that he forgot he had cheat sheets with him.

Professor Verma walked up to Venky and Vikas to check on their progress. Since both of them were good students, he didn't expect them to face any problem.

'Gentlemen, hope all is well.'

'Yes sir. I've connected the source and I am observing the output now. Things seem fine.'

Professor Verma looked around and walked away. As he moved away, he saw a piece of paper lying on the ground. He picked it up to see what it was. He saw a circuit diagram on it. Immediately, his invigilator mind suspected something fishy. He turned around and stood next to Venky.

'What is this?'

Venky was shocked to see the cheat sheet in Professor Verma's hand. Venky couldn't say anything. He just stood there transfixed.

Professor Verma said sternly, 'Show me your pockets.'

The professor put his hands into Venky's pant pocket and pulled out the cheat sheets.

'Sir, sir, I was not cheating.'

'What is all this? Come out of the hall immediately.'

Venky was at his wits' end as he realized his folly. Outside the exam hall, Professor Verma looked at the sheets carefully and found that they were not handwritten, but photocopied.

'These are photocopied! I can't believe this. So, that means there are others out there.'

The professor quickly went back to the class room.

'All of you immediately stop the exam.'

Professor Verma's eyes quickly scanned through the room looking for the others. A fleeting contact with the eyes of the others was enough for him to know who they were.

The students knew their game was up and they started to take the cheat sheets out of their pockets and put them on the table.

'Leave the examination hall immediately.'

Saahil, Vikas, Rajeev and Dinesh walked out of the classroom.

Standing outside the hall looking at the others complete the examination was embarrassing.

Professor Verma walked up to them and said, 'Meet me in my room in ten minutes.'

The five entered his room.

'I'm very disappointed. How could you even think of doing this nonsense?' screamed Professor Verma.

He then rang the bell and called the peon.

The peon walked in with sheets of paper and put them on Professor Verma's desk. He glanced through them quickly and motioned to the five students to take them. Everyone looked at Venky and nudged him.

Even before they could read it properly, the professor commanded, 'Each of you sign this.'

They looked at each other with a shocked expression.

Venky distributed the sheets to the group.

They glanced at the sheet quickly and knew it was trouble.

'Sir, we are very sorry,' said all of them in a chorus. Prof. Verma was in no mood to listen to them.

'If you don't sign this letter, I will be rusticating you from the course. If you sign it, I will send it to the university as an unfair means case and the maximum punishment is you will be debarred from taking the exams for three years. The choice is yours.'

They gulped and cleared their throats, trying to digest what the professor had said.

All of them signed the document and walked out. They reached the hostel to find a huge crowd in the canteen sitting and chatting. It was obvious that they were discussing this incident.

A few of them approached them and asked them what happened. They were pleasantly surprised by the support they got. Though they could not do much, having them around was consoling.

None of them could sleep well that night. It seemed liked the end of the road for them. If they couldn't give the exams for three years, their career was over. In India, where fresh engineers came out of an assembly line every year, who would be interested in defective pieces like them?

Each one of them painted a picture of their gloomy future.

Saahil could see himself starting a bike rental and repair shop. Venky saw himself taking tuitions for students. Vikas could see himself running his father's air conditioning business in Ludhiana. For Dinesh, the future seemed so terrifying that sleep seemed a better option.

The next morning, the five of them got together and went out for breakfast like a bunch of outcasts. They couldn't understand whether they should attend classes or not.

All of them decided to bunk classes and be on their own. The whole day passed by and they seemed to be only getting more depressed by the thought of what awaited them.

In the evening, they were sitting in the canteen sipping tea and cursing each other, especially Venky for landing them in this mess.

Saahil walked up to them. 'Guys, I'm going to the temple. Want to come along?'

All of them looked at each other, astonished at what they'd heard. Saahil, the biker dude, remembered God almighty only when his bike broke down or when he had to take a girl out on a date.

But now only a miracle could save them. So, seeking divine intervention seemed appropriate to Saahil and the others.

Vikas's eye caught something familiar in the temple. Prof. Verma was leaving with his family on a scooter after offering prayers.

Vikas knew where Prof. Verma lived so took the other boys to his house. He rang the bell and Prof. Verma's wife came out to see who it was.

'Good evening, ma'am. We are Prof. Verma's students. Can we please meet him?' said Vikas confidently. Five minutes later, Prof. Verma appeared and walked up to the gate of his house.

Opening the gate, he said, 'Why don't you all come in?'

Seeing this gesture, they were a little relieved.

Vikas led the group. He gave the professor some prasad (offerings from the deity).

Prof. Verma asked them all to sit down in his drawing room and asked, 'So, what can I do for you?'

Vikas took the lead and said, 'Sir, we actually were not cheating. We brought the chits but did not use them. Actually, we found the exam quite easy.' The others were ready to laugh at the stark dichotomy of his statement but restrained themselves.

Vikas continued with his emotional speech fortified with histrionics. Saahil wanted to stop Vikas from going overboard but he seemed too busy trying out his acting skills as a possible second career option.

Prof. Verma looked at him and simply uttered, 'Hmm.'

Vikas looked at Saahil who took the baton and started, 'Sir, please don't send the letter to the authorities. Our careers will be ruined. Sir, we are very sorry.'

Prof. Verma just looked at them and then turned around and said, 'Kavita, is the tea ready?'

'Yes, just bringing it,' replied his wife.

'The letters have already been dispatched as per procedure. In a few weeks you will find out the committee's final verdict.'

The boys somehow gulped their tea and were on their way to the hostel.

For the next ten days, hostellers would see a group of five students soberly dressed, walking out of the campus. On their return, this bunch would offer prasad to everyone and then go to their rooms. The trips to the temple continued, as the boys kept hoping for a miracle.

They resumed their classes but the sword of uncertainty was still hanging on their heads. The rest of the class started excluding them from the usual discussions on the annual day function and campus placements.

During a practical class, when the boys were sitting and trying to work out the results, the office attendant walked up to them asking them to meet the dean.

They went to the dean's chamber to find Prof. Verma already there.

The director, Dr Vishesh Adhikari, looked at all of them and said, 'It is shameful that you all have dared to do this despicable act.

I'm disappointed in each of you. Remember this, whether you succeed or fail in life is not important. What's important are the means you choose. The world will judge you on your successes and your failures. But only you know the path you have chosen. Be true to yourself.'

The dean looked at Prof. Verma.

Prof. Verma said, 'You will have to take a retest in your practicals. In your main paper, you will be given just pass marks. We are forgiving you this time. But don't take this lightly.'

He got up and walked out to his chamber.

The students couldn't believe their ears and heaved a sigh of relief.

Prof. Verma looked at them and said 'This better not happen again. And one last thing, you were not let off because of your trips to the temple. Consider this as your second life.'

Thanking their luck, they walked back to the hostel.

Venky told the others that he would join them later at the hostel. He wanted to walk up to the lake near the college.

Venky liked walking up to the lake on weekends. But today, as he approached the lake, it seemed different. It appeared dark and grey, instead of the usual serene light blue. Further down from where Venky was standing, he could see a bunch of kids merrily throwing stones in the water. He walked up to them. They barely noticed his presence and continued to play, challenging each other to throw the farthest and make the stones bounce on the water surface.

Venky walked up to the youngest kid and knelt down next to him. The kid looked at the stranger with shyness and confusion.

Putting his arms around the kid and looking straight into his eyes, Venky said to him, 'Be true to yourself. Hmm… Remember this.'

The kid gave Venky a confused look.

***

'Venky, I can bet after this incident you didn't even go near a photocopy shop,' said Shivam thumping the table.

'If it's up to me, I'll ban the use of photocopiers for eternity,' laughed Venky.

'I'm famished,' said Shivam and called the waiter. He took the lead and ordered dishes to suit everyone's preferences.

'Please make sure the Castelvetrano olives are not too salty,' he added, smiling at the waiter.

Everyone was impressed to see the food connoisseur that Shivam had become.

Nafisa asked, 'Should we call the waiter to decide who's going next?'

Before Nafisa did that, Francis raised his hand.

DEEP END

Every evening, after college, Francis made it a point to swim at the university pool. One summer evening, as he was doing the laps at the Olympic-size pool, he saw two very athletic guys jump into the pool. He took a break and watched them easily complete lap after lap in the pool. Then he saw the coach come by. The coach was a tall well-built oak who looked more like a wrestler than a swimmer. He ordered the guys to do intense pull-ups by the poolside.

Looking at Francis, the coach shouted in his strong Haryanvi accent, 'Why don't you also do some of these?'

Francis didn't want to look like a weakling. So, he tried a few pull-ups. He had barely managed a few when his whole body began to shake. The coach walked up to him and looked him straight in the eyes and said, 'You have a good swimming style but that is not enough. You also need stamina and strong muscles. Inter-college water polo matches start next month. I'm building a team and I want you to be on it.'

Francis was happy that the coach had noticed his swimming style.

'Sir, I would love to but I don't know how to play water polo,' replied Francis excitedly.

'Don't worry. If I throw a monkey into the deep end with a ball, even he'll learn water polo. You are a good swimmer, you'll learn fast. Don't forget you will get an inter-college certificate; so, work hard.'

Francis got all pumped up to participate in the competition.

For the next month, the coach made Francis train hard on the game. Occasionally, the other players, Kartik and Vinod, from the law department, also practiced with Francis.

A month passed by quickly. Soon it was match day. Francis excused himself from the classes and arrived at the pool half an hour before the match for his warm-up. Francis's only concern was he had seen only Kartik and Vinod practice; he had no idea who the other four in the team were.

When he reached the stadium, Francis saw five beefy guys practicing their water polo shots. Francis shouted out to them.

One of the guys waved back at him and said, 'Come, join us.'

Francis dove into the pool. He felt the power of the other boys as they passed the ball to him. They were over six feet tall with bodies that would make even the best gym rats envious. The manner in which they were leaping out of the water and throwing the ball made Francis think they would make India proud at the Olympics someday. Talent, sheer talent, is what these guys had. They also had a common surname. They were Gurjeet Singh, Neetu Singh, Balvinder Singh, Jagjit Singh and Lucky Singh.

Francis wished these guys had come for the earlier training sessions, so that they could have practiced together. But the match was about to start and there was not much they could do now. The opposing team was from the neighbouring state. Though they seemed athletic, they were nothing compared to the burly five from Mathewson.

The fifty-meter pool had a partition in the middle. One goal post was in the middle of the pool and the other was at the deep end.

The captain, Kartik, walked up to his team and said, 'Let's decide the team for the first jump.' Francis volunteered to sit out for the first jump. He could already see himself walking back to the hostel with the certificate.

The referees checked the nails of all the swimmers and gave the go-ahead for the match to start.

Mathewson College was in the middle of the pool and Tejgarh State College was in the deep end.

At the first whistle, swimmers from both the teams swam to take possession of the ball floating in the centre of the court. Kartik was the fastest among all the players. He quickly got to the ball and flicked it back into his court towards Jagjit. Jagjit returned the ball to Kartik who had already reached the goal post. With one swift action, Kartik leaped and slammed the ball into the goal post. The ball flew through the air but before it could kiss the net, the opponent goalkeeper's fist punched it out of the pool. Kartik was disappointed at the missed chance.

The opponent goalkeeper then passed the ball to the defender. The defender swam from the left flank and, with a deft back hand pass, threw the ball to the striker on the right flank who smoothly lifted his body out of the water and thumped the ball into the goal. Lucky Singh, the goalkeeper, was left blinking.

A few seconds later, before he could blink again, the ball came crashing back into the net, and within few minutes another goal was shot and then another one. At the end of the first quarter, the score was 4–0 against Mathewson.

Francis was shocked to see what was happening. He walked up to

Kartik who was at the side pool catching some breath. He asked him angrily, 'Why are most of the players huddled in our side? To score, we need to be on the opponent's side. Right?'

Kartik replied, 'None of these fellows are good swimmers.'

Francis asked with a confused look, 'What do you mean?'

'They are from the university's wrestling team.'

'What! Are you kidding me? Then why the hell are they here?'

'The same reason that you are here. For the certificate. Now, get ready to take a jump in the next quarter.'

Francis couldn't believe his ears. Now it made sense as to why the burly guys kept going back to their half. The water was not that deep and their feet could easily touch the floor of the pool.

Just then, the whistle for the next quarter went off.

Francis brought the team together and said, 'Guys, we need to make a match of this somehow.'

Earlier, the Singhs had not been able to stand in the deep side of the pool. But after the side switch, they were all now on the shallow side of the pool, which was close to opponent's goal post. Francis knew this would spell disaster because now they had no one in the defence.

The guys from Tejgarh were equally shocked to see most of the Mathewson Technical College swimmers on their side.

The whistle blew and the Tejgarh attackers went on the offensive again; this time they saw an unguarded goal post.

At the end of two quarters, the score was 8–0.

Slowly, word got around that the home team was playing a water polo match. People gathered around to cheer for their local team. But they were stunned to see their team performing so badly.

During the break, at the end of the quarter, Francis sat with his hand between his knees, trying to catch some breath.

Kartik got out of the water in a big huff.

'Let's huddle quickly,' he said.

All the wrestlers sheepishly tried to form a circle. Kartik was waiting for Francis to join them but he didn't bother calling him again.

Kartik lost his patience as he said, 'Guys, were you thinking that playing water polo was a cakewalk? That you would walk out of your wrestling pits and walk away with a water polo certificate?'

Balvinder Singh retorted, 'But we swam in our village pond and thought all we had to do was to throw the ball around. Anyway, all we want is the participation certificate.'

Kartik was starting to lose his cool with his men. He was not bothered that they were bigger than him in size.

'Hope you now know the difference between swimming in a village pond and playing competitive water polo. You all are a major embarrassment. Now, you guys will shut up and listen to what I say. We have the last two rounds quarters left and we need to score goals. Do you guys know how to do the doggy paddle?'

The wrestlers had a stunned look on their face.

'Okay, cup your hands like this and wave them vigorously underwater while moving your legs in a cycling motion. Now, does this make sense?'

They nodded their heads, but no one knew whether they understood what Kartik was saying.

'Most of you will defend; only Francis, Jagjit and I will attack. The rest of the defenders will mark their men. Balvinder and Neetu, you guys have strong arms but you are very poor swimmers. So, just stay at the back and pass the ball in front. And remember, I don't want any more goals against us.'

Francis was listening to the talk but he was too dejected to participate in it. Only towards the end, he walked up to the circle to see Kartik, who was barely five-feet tall, berate the bulky men. Seeing this gave him some confidence.

Putting his hand on Kartik's shoulder, Francis said, 'Let's make a match out of this, captain.' He kissed the cross around his neck and jumped into the water.

The whistle for the third quarter blew and Kartik made a strong sprint towards the ball. Everyone could see the captain charged up. He reached the ball before the opponents could and passed it to Balvinder. Balvinder used all his muscle to throw the ball towards the opponent's goal post. Francis then made a quick pass to Kartik, but before he could collect the ball, the defender dived straight in front and passed it to the striker. Before Balvinder and Neetu could understand what happened, the ball sailed through them, caressing the net. Lucky Singh, the goalkeeper, shouted at them, 'What the hell are you two doing?'

The score was now 9–0.

The crowd, which had filled the stadium in large numbers, was disgusted with the home team's performance. The match was a joke.

A girl from the university women hockey team remarked, 'These guys are not even fit to play with us.' Another girl shouted at the team, 'Didn't your mummy give you any breakfast today?'

Kartik urged his team, 'C'mon boys, don't lose heart. It's not over yet. Balvinder, your throw was very good. We need more of those long passes.'

Kartik was on the offensive. This time, instead of passing across the flanks, he asked Francis to stay with him on the left flank, which looked weaker. They passed the ball to each other and made good ground. Just then, one of the opponents whacked Francis on his back. His hand landed with such ferocity that he nearly was knocked out. But Francis gained composure and somehow managed to pass the ball to Kartik. Kartik caught hold of the ball and dodged past a defender. There was now only one defender between him and the keeper.

Francis swam hard and sneaked next to Kartik. Kartik turned around and passed the ball to Francis who swam passed the defender. Francis swiftly passed the ball over the defender's head to Kartik, who smashed the ball into the net.

The audience broke into a loud and wild roar as if it was the winning goal.

The home team had finally scored its first goal.

With the score reading 9–1, the whistle blew again for the last five minutes.

The opponent team's captain shouted out to his players, 'Let's make it ten.'

This time Kartik had a different plan. He called everyone for a huddle.

'Make a wall,' Kartik told his team.

The Mathewson players lined up in two files to thwart the final assault from the opponent. The Singhs doggy paddled insanely to stay afloat in the same place. Though they were hopelessly out of breath and their eyes were smarting due to the chlorine in the water, they were determined not to let their captain down.

The opponents made several attempts to score in the dying minutes of the game. But the wall was impregnable. The captain's strategy had worked. The referee blew the final whistle and the match ended at 9–1.

The winning team was ecstatic. They formed a circle putting their arm around each other and were shouting wildly.

The home team shook hands with the winners and quickly ran back to their change rooms to avoid the jeering crowd.

Francis saw the coach walking towards them but he was in no mood to talk to anyone. He quickly changed his clothes and bolted towards the hostel.

Instead of using the main entrance, he jumped across the wall and tip-toed to his room hoping not to bump into anybody in the corridor.

***

'Francis, I wish this match was played now. It would have become the funniest video of all time,' said Harpreet laughing.

'True that,' joined Aadil.

'Folks, time for me to call it a night. You guys enjoy the evening,' announced Francis getting up.

'Francis, you are ditching us buddy. We were to stay till the last order,' said Harpreet getting up and hugging Francis.

Francis also hugged Harpreet and winked at the others indicating how drunk Harpreet was now.

Harpreet was in no mood to let Francis go.

'Okay, okay, Harpreet. Let go. I'm staying.'

Harpreet sat back down with a thud and looking philosophically at the ceiling said, 'I miss Joginder's parathas.'

The others looked at each other and nodded.

'Forget picking up a mobile phone this time. Let me go next,' said Aadil in his unchanged self-assured style.

ZEN AND MAGGI

It was 1a.m. when Sameer got up from his desk to get water for the third time in two hours. Though he'd bribed the hostel staff to make sure he got a room that was not sun-facing, the daytime heat was so much that even in the nights there was no respite. Summers were undoubtedly the worst time to be in a hostel in northern India. Walking towards the water cooler at the end of the corridor, Sameer was wondering about the strategy to scrape through the semester exam the next day.

He wondered how he had got himself into such a mess. Just then images of him waving his cricket bat after hitting fours sixes to win a bet surfaced in his mind.

On the way to the water cooler, Sameer heard sounds from Deepak's room. 'You can do it Deepak, come on.'

'Yeah Deepak, you can do it,' shouted Sameer with a big laugh and kept walking.

Before he reached the cooler, Sameer was distracted by the light from Aadil's room.

Sameer gave a hard kick on the door and was shocked to see Aadil lying down on the bed in his underwear reading Zen and the Art of Motorcycle Maintenance and slurping Maggi noodles. His bed was surrounded by two inches of water he had filled to keep the room cool in summers. Aadil's face wore a blissful expression.

Aadil reminded Sameer of the Hindu god, Lord Vishnu, who is always depicted sitting on the five-headed serpent, Ananta-Shesha, floating on the ocean.

'You bastard! You are sitting and reading some nonsensical book before the electronics exam? Have you gone mad?' screamed Sameer. He forded the water and snatched the bowl of Maggi from Aadil. Aadil gave it to Sameer without any resistance and continued reading.

'Looks like you've finished the course,' said Sameer, slurping some of the piping hot noodles.

'No,' replied Aadil coolly.

'How many more chapters to go?'

'All.'

'Are you serious? What's the plan?'

'Repeat the exam.'

'But why?'

'It's complex. Very complex. You won't get it. So, don't waste your time.'

'Oh yeah? Shut-up and tell me what you're up to.'

'I'm doing an experiment'

'What experiment?'

'I believe our education system makes us conformists which I think is not good in the long run. Just think what are we doing sitting in their rooms today. Cramming for an exam to compete rather than to learn. Is that what will help us in the future? I don't think so. I'm not giving the exam tomorrow. I'll give it when I'm ready. To do spectacular work you need to be inspired, not coerced.'

'Hmm, that's deep. Very deep. What have you been drinking?'

'A tasteless, odourless liquid called H2O. You must try it sometime.'

'You've got a point about inspiration but that is not enough for excellence. At least not in an engineering college. There's another element you need. Girls,' Sameer said and sat down on Aadil's bed looking dejected.

'Ha ha! Looks like you've been ditched again,' said Aadil, laughing at Sameer's perspective.

'There are always such few girls in engineering college. You agree?

'Yeah, maybe less than two per cent. So?'

'So, when there are such few girls around, you spend half your time fantasizing about them. If you spend half your time in unproductive work, how do you expect to do anything worthwhile?'

'Interesting problem statement.'

Aadil got up, snatched the bowl of noodles back from Sameer and opened the door to his balcony. The warm air hit their faces.

Aadil looked at Sameer with a strange expression and said, 'This problem may have a solution. A technology solution.'

Sameer could sense excitement in Aadil's voice and knew something mind-blowing was coming.

'Look Sameer! Your problem is that you are only seeing the girls in our batch. But there a lot of girls in other departments and colleges in the city. Right?'

'Okay, but I don't have the time going around the city trying to meet them. I don't want to flunk.'

'Ok, but this is where the internet comes in. Today the internet is a new concept but believe me it's the future. We'll create a website.'

'Okay. But explain what this site will do?'

This website will allow boys and girls from different colleges to interact with each other. Why restrict yourself to the girls of your college?'

'I know there's an internet boom but don't you think there are already too many websites out there…'

'Hear me out. I'm not finished yet. Do you think people just want to chat? Online chatting is good but not that great. You want to meet girls, have coffee with them, go out for a movie with them, and make others jealous. Online chat is virtual. It's not the real deal.'

'Yes, chat engines have their limitations.'

'So, the idea is to have a real interaction.'

'Sounds cool.'

'Now wait for the best part. Meetings can be expensive. A student can burn a hole in his pocket with the price in coffee shops and restaurants. Not many students can afford that. So, to solve that problem, we can provide discounts to couples. We can tie up with restaurants and cafes who would be happy to see the traffic coming in,' said Aadil, delivering the USP of his pitch.

'I think we have a winning business model here,' said Sameer, starting to feel convinced about the idea.

Aadil was in no mood to stop.

'Hey Sameer. Let's ride down to our favourite trucker's eatery on the highway and continue brainstorming.'

'Yes let's do that. But first put on your jeans. I hope you don't intend to ride your bike in your underwear otherwise you'll become the talk of the girls' hostel', said Sameer with a wink.

'Actually, I wouldn't mind that', replied Aadil wearing his worn-out jeans.

At the trucker's eatery, they ordered their favourite cream buns and discussed various aspects related to the idea. They were both convinced with the idea and started preparing a rough business plan. Aadil and Sameer were so engrossed in planning that they didn't notice there were only a couple of hours left before the exam. When they realized they were out of time, they stopped their discussion and quickly went back to the hostel.

Sameer asked Aadil, 'Are you serious about missing the exam?'

'Exams can be repeated. But one doesn't get inspired every day.'

***

'I remember you guys built that website. What happened after that? Did it take off? asked Nafisa

'Oh yes it did take off. In fact, it became quite a hit', replied Harpreet.

'This is interesting. I didn't know this.'

Aadil winked at Harpreet indicating him not to speak further. But Nafisa saw him do that.

'Hey Aadil why are you stopping Harpreet. This is not fair guys. I want to know what happened.'

'Okay. So Nafisa, if you are so interested, here it is.'

MOHABBAT.COM

Rahul entered Aadil's room late one night. It was in a mess. In one corner Aadil had somehow managed to squeeze in a desktop computer. In the other corner, there was his bed strewn with second-hand books on computers.

'Are you serious about making that website?', asked Rahul

Aadil looked up at Rahul and went back to feverishly typing on his hired desktop.

Rahul coolly walked to up to Aadil's cupboard popped two coconut laddoos and quietly walked out the room. On any other day, Aadil would have skinned him alive for laying hands on his favourite midnight snack.

Sameer initially tried to wriggle out of this seemingly crazy idea but Aadil made sure he couldn't escape.

Every evening after dinner they could be seen taking a walk around the campus discussing some issue or other related to Mohabbat.com.

After two months of toil, Aadil and Sameer were ready to test the website. They nervously tested it but were happy to see that the basic website was working. Now was the difficult part of getting people to register on it.

Since computers were not yet allowed in hostel rooms the only way people could register on the site was from University cyber cafes.

They first approached the girls from their own college. Some girls listened to them but somehow felt there was something fishy and didn't register. Others would just giggle when they heard the name of the site. Despite of their best efforts, Aadil and Sameer struggled to get people to register on the site.

Nothing was going well for Aadil. To make matters worse, Aadil got into a fight with Ashraf from the senior batch when he opposed him in the mess election. Aadil supported Ashraf's batchmate Talvinder Singh. Talvinder was one of the most popular seniors in the hostel. He was popular because he took juniors on his bike to all the famous street food eateries in the city.

His love for food was legendary. During ragging, Talvinder had become notorious for asking all juniors to first stop at his room, empty their stock of snacks and sweets before he allowed them to go to their rooms.

It was during one of these ragging sessions that Talvinder and Aadil had hit it off well. Talvinder became of a fan of his home-made poori and naan khatai and thereafter gave him the nickname Mithaiwala Parsi Baba.

Talvinder and Ashraf were locked in a fierce battle to win the elections.

When Ashraf found out that Aadil was campaigning aggressively for Talvinder, he confronted him in front of everyone and asked him to stay away from the elections.

Ashraf and Alok were regulars outside the girls' hostel. Often just waiting for a chance to talk to the girls on some pretext or the other. Ashraf had a crush on Nafisa and wanted to ask her out on a date. But every time he tried to approach her either he would chicken out or Nafisa would brush him aside.

One morning Alok was shaving in the boys' hostel bathroom when he noticed Sameer shaving next to him.

'What happened? How come you are on this floor?', asked Alok.

'No water on our floor,' replied Sameer and continued shaving.

'That's strange.'

After a while Alok asked Sameer,' So, how is your dating website coming along?'

'Actually, coming along quite well. Registrations have been great. A lot of guys and girls have already starting dating using the website. The best part is even girls from outside the college have registered.'

'I don't believe it. It must be mostly guys. I don't believe that girls from our college would register. You are bullshitting me,' challenged Alok.

'Don't believe me? Come to my room and I'll show you the profiles,' retorted Sameer.

'Okay. Give me a few names then and I'll check-out their profiles'

'You know Sandhya from the 1st batch? She's there. Prachi from your batch registered. Even Nafisa from our batch is on it,' said Sameer as he finished shaving.

'Hmm interesting. I didn't know Nafisa is the dating type. She looks so studious.'

***

Later, during the day, when Alok and Ashraf were returning to the hostel

'Dude, guess what! I was speaking to Sameer and he said that Nafisa has registered on the website,' Alok informed Ashraf.

'What are you saying? Man, I will do anything to go out on a date with her just once. I'll register today and ask her out on a date,' said Ashraf excitedly.

'Good idea bro', said Alok supporting Ashraf.

That evening, Ashraf and Alok went to the cybercafé in the market and created their profiles.

Ashraf sent a message to Nafisa 'Hey Nafisa. Let's be friends.'

For the next couple of weeks, both Ashraf and Alok would religiously go to the cybercafé to check their Mohabbat.com profile. But there was no response from Nafisa.

One Friday evening Ashraf, Alok, Sanjay and the others were drinking in the hostel room. Very soon the discussion moved to everyone's favourite topic—girls.

'Ashraf, I heard that you asked Nafisa out on a date but she refused', said Vikas taking a swig from the beer bottle.

'What rubbish. She'll go out on a date with me. She just taking her time,' replied Ashraf

'I don't think she's interested in you. You should give up.'

'I'll prove to you that she'll send me a reply.'

'Okay. If you are so confident. Why don't we go and check now? Maybe she's already sent you a reply,' Sanjay provoked him.

Ashraf was not at all interested but since Sanjay and the others were insisting, he was left with no choice.

They realized that the only cybercafé that would be open at this hour would be the one outside the University that catered to research scholars.

They got on their scooters and reached there to find three studious students engrossed in their research. With a straight face they walked up to the owner and asked him for a computer.

Ashraf knew that there was practically no chance that there would be message from Nafisa but since he had been cornered, he put up a brave face.

'Go to your account,' insisted Sanjay.

Ashraf reluctantly logged into the account. Alok quickly looked at the screen and shouted, 'Click here.'

Ashraf squinted his eyes to see the number one flashing on the Inbox icon. He was worried about the content of the message but clicked the icon nonetheless.

'Hi Ashraf, Great to hear from you. Few girls from the hostel are planning to watch the movie Kareeb at Bharat Talkies so we thought it would be great if you could also join us. Meet us at market outside Pushkar Juice stall at 2p.m.'

Look forward to seeing you.

Nafisa'

Ashraf couldn't believe it got up and shouted 'I told you. I told you. She'll respond.'

Sanjay and the others found it hard to digest but they had to accept that Ashraf really was The Man.

The research scholars gave them annoyed looks and got back to their reading.

Ashraf couldn't sleep the whole night. He was already picturing himself sitting next to Nafisa holding her hand.

The next day Ashraf, Atul and Sanjay were ready to meet the girls at the market. They kept the news to themselves and made sure nobody got wind of this development.

Casually, the three of them got onto their bikes and reached the market. Though some of the fellow hostellers found it unusual to see these three so well dressed in the afternoon, they didn't pay much heed.

The market was mostly deserted. Three of them reached fifteen minutes early and were planning who would sit next to which girl during the film. The girls were to come in their scooters which they would park and then go with the boys.

They were busy chatting when they glanced at their watches, it was already 2. 30p.m. They were wondering what was taking the girls so long.

To while away time, they thought of ordering some fruit juice.

'Three large orange juices with masala,' said Ashraf to the shop-keeper.

They were picking up their glasses from the shopkeeper's assistant when they heard the sound of scooters in the background.

They turned around expecting to see the girls, but that was not to be.

Talvinder and Aakash were sitting on their scooter and laughing loudly at Ashraf and his gang.

'Ashraf, there's space on my scooter. Come I'll take you to the movie,' said Talvinder with a laugh and sped away leaving Ashraf and his gang red faced.

***

'Can't believe you guys created my fake profile and conned Ashraf,' said Nafisa with amazement.

'Thanks to your popularity among the boys, at least we were able to set-up a date through Mohabbat.com, even if it was a fake one,' said Aadil.

'Popularity? I was hardly the type!'

'You have no idea how many fans you had in the boy's hostel.'

'Oh please, if having fans like Ashraf means being popular, I'm better off without them.'

'No, no. You had many fans besides Ashraf.'

Nafisa ignored the statement.

Raghav who was silent all this while, picked up his glass and looked at the others. The others looked at each other a bit surprised but obliged him nonetheless. Raghav clinked his glass with that of the others and said, 'I'll tell you my story now.'

MURPHY'S LAW

Cricket ground, Diwan Chand Institute

Sujoy was padded up, awaiting his turn to bat. He was the captain of the Mathewson cricket team and was proud that they'd reached the finals of the Annual State Cricket Tournament for the first time, against arch rivals Diwan Chand College. Diwan Chand had scored 168 in their twenty overs. It was a good score, but the way Vikrant and Vinay were batting, he could already picture himself celebrating their victory in Lucky Sweet Shop.

'This over, let's play safe,' said Vikrant to Vinay and got ready to take strike against the big burly fast bowler from Diwan Chand College. The bowler came around the wicket and bowled a screeching yorker. Vikrant misjudged the length completely. The screaming of the fielders around was enough to tell him that he had been clean-bowled.

Walking on the pitch and taking guard, Sujoy felt confident. The bowler ran up confidently hoping to bowl the same ball, but it turned out to be a full toss. Sujoy swung his bat and the ball flew towards the offside boundary. But instead of crossing the boundary, it landed safely in the hands of the fielder. Sujoy couldn't believe it. He was out on a duck when his team had needed him the most.

Diwan Chand lifted the trophy for the fifth time in a row.

Two semesters had passed since Sujoy had lost the match, but even now, every time the autorickshaw passed the Diwan Chand ground, memories of that day came rushing back into his head. 'Why didn't I just settle down instead of swinging my bat at the first ball?' lamented Sujoy.

It was a cold February morning and the early morning train pulled into the railway station. Sujoy quickly picked up his rucksack and jumped onto the platform. Dodging the passengers, coolies and caterers, Sujoy rushed to find an autorickshaw that would take him to the university. He found one with just one seat vacant. He quickly jumped in.

Sujoy's mind was preoccupied with the upcoming placement season. The buzz in the market was that this was going to be a good year. He imagined himself being interviewed by a top engineering firm, when he was interrupted by the words 'fashion show'.

The two girls in the auto were talking excitedly about a fashion show that was going to be held during their college festival. He tried to follow their conversation; he figured out that they were from none other than Diwan Chand College. By the time the auto reached the college gates, the girls had discussed almost everything under the sun.

Sujoy got off outside his hostel gate and continued thinking about the upcoming placements.

***

One evening at the hostel canteen, a visibly agitated Dinesh said, 'What's happened to Professor Shukla? Doesn't he know we are in the last semester and we need to prepare for the placements? He still keeps insisting on attendance. I think, with my poor attendance, I'm going to flunk his paper.'

Raghav was in a particularly pensive mood that evening. He said, 'I can't believe that four years are about to pass. Four freaking long years and all we did was study like mules.'

Francis also joined the conversation. 'Seriously, sometimes I regret not having planned better. When I joined college, I told myself that I would religiously work out and swim every day. I even went and bought books that I had planned to read. But all I've done is stare at those books, every single day of the last four years of my life.'

Sujoy, who had been listening to the conversation, said, 'Guys, if you want to do something that you haven't done before, here's our chance.'

'What do you mean?' asked Raghav.

'Diwan Chand's annual festival has a fashion show event this year. Let's participate.'

Raghav detested the idea. 'Fashion show! Doing this tomfoolery when the placement season is around the corner! Are you stupid? In the placements, what are they going to ask us? Let us know what you wore in the ethnic round?'

'Your choice, Raghav. But remember, twenty years down the line, it will not matter that you aced every single exam in the course. But what will matter are the experiences you had.'

Raghav and Francis looked at each other and got up. They knew that Sujoy had hit the nail on its head.

A few days later, when Sujoy was returning to his hostel after giving his viva test, he bumped into Vandana.

'Where have you been? We've been looking for you at the canteen. Come on.'

'Hmm. That's strange. I don't remember owing people any money,' said Sujoy.

When Sujoy reached the canteen, he saw several tables had been joined together and the students were crowded around them discussing something fervently.

As Sujoy was looking for a place to sit, Aarti asked him, 'So Sujoy, what do you think should be the theme for the fashion show?'

Sujoy was a bit confused, 'Whoa… what fashion show?'

Just then, Raghav walked in and patted him on the back. 'Dude, let's make our last year count.'

Sujoy couldn't believe it. In fact, Raghav had managed to convince many others that they had to make their last year worthwhile, though they were still a bit hesitant about participating in a fashion show. After a few days of sweet-talking, cajoling, convincing and terrorizing folks, Sujoy was able to get together a team to participate in the event.

One morning, Aadil woke up as usual and walked out on the corridor where he saw the canteen boy with his aluminium kettle and cups.

'Give me a cup, please,' said Aadil, still half asleep.

Aadil took his tea and picked up the newspaper lying outside his room. He then walked out onto the balcony of his room and started flipping through the pages of the newspaper when something caught his eye. He looked down at the ground below and saw a weird-looking structure.

It was a brick outlined T-shaped structure with a rectangle at the bottom. Before he could rack his brain further, he saw Raghav walking on the structure counting out numbers loudly, as if he was on a ramp.

Aadil called out to Raghav, 'What the hell are you doing?' Without bothering to look up, Raghav replied, 'Can't you see you, moron? I'm walking on a ramp.' Aadil's eyes followed Raghav as he completed the walk on his practice 'ramp.'

***

The team of seventeen was split into a group of models, choreographers and logistics personnel. A slot of two hours every day was allotted for practice.

On the first day, the boys and the girls sat in their own groups, waiting for someone to take the lead. Sujoy was lost, but he quickly composed himself to take charge. He had come up with the idea and he had to make sure things moved smoothly. There was no looking back now.

He got up to address the bunch of students.

'Friends, a big thank you for volunteering to participate in this year's annual function at Diwan Chand College. I've never modelled even in front of a mirror, forget walking on the ramp. But here's our opportunity to challenge ourselves to do something different, something we've never done before. We must push ourselves out of our comfort zone. I'm sure that if we work together, we stand a good chance of winning.'

The ensuing silence was broken by the faint noise of a few students clapping. Sujoy could see that the motivation was abysmally low. He had to do better.

***

For the next few days, the team practiced vigorously on their 'La Fusion' theme for the Navyata fashion show. 'Navyata' meant 'fashion' in Sanskrit. It was easily the highlight event of the annual college festival.

When D-day arrived, the Mathewson team arrived at the venue in small groups. They were impressed by the arrangements that had been made. The venue had been beautifully lit. There was separate seating for the VIPs, faculty and students. Since it was the most sought-after event, there were hardly any empty seats. Sujoy had barely gotten off the scooter when an event organizer rushed to him and asked him to get ready for the event.

As luck would have it, the Mathewson team had to go in first. But the entire team hadn't yet arrived.

Sujoy told the organizer that they would need fifteen minutes.

Nervously Sujoy asked Raghav, 'Where are the others?'

Raghav looked a little confused as he said, 'Hmm. Good question.'

'Get ready quickly, you have only fifteen minutes.'

Suddenly, Raghav tapped Sujoy lightly and pointed in the distance, 'Look there.'

Sujoy strained his eyes in the darkness and exclaimed, 'What the hell is that?'

At a distance, they could see two scooters approaching them with something shimmering. It was the girls decked up in their borrowed bridal finery.

Nafisa parked her scooter and said, 'Sorry guys! We realized very late that none of us knew how to wear a sari. Finally, the hostel's lady warden helped us out.'

Raghav said, 'Okay, now listen. We are going in first.' The girls shrieked hysterically as if Salman Khan had announced his wedding.

Nafisa looked at the other girls with a serious face, 'Girls, we don't have too much time for make-up now.'

The guys were about to faint when they heard this but they somehow composed themselves.

Just then, the organizer came back and shrieked at them 'Mathewson College, you are delaying the show. Start immediately!'

The emcee soon made an announcement and the Mathewson team was up on the ramp for the first round—the ethnic outfits round. The team members looked at each other to assess the level of nervousness. Raghav glanced at Nafisa and wondered how she managed to look so stunning. Raghav was about to wish her luck, but before he could, he felt a big push from behind.

Rajat shouted, 'The music has started. Get on the ramp.'

As they stepped on the ramp, they were shocked to hear the Bryan Adams song '18 till I die' playing in the ethnic round. All of them exchanged shocked glances and even a few expletives. How did this happen? Why was Aadil not able to get this simple thing right?

The men were nattily dressed in sherwani, churidar kurta and dhoti. The women complemented them very well with beautiful sarees from different Indian states. They managed to walk the ramp with panache, forgetting that the music was a mismatch. The round ended with the two main couples bowing gracefully with their hands folded.

In the background, Aadil was livid. He was shouting at the event organizers.

'Hey, what the heck were you doing?' shouted Aadil. 'This was the song for the next round.'

The audio manager from Diwan Chand College replied apologetically, 'Oh, okay! I think the music got switched.' The manner in which things were being handled, Aadil felt the mix-up may have been intentional.

The models got back quickly into their changing rooms to get ready for the sports attire round. They hardly spoke to each other.

After wishing each other good luck, the team went on stage again. The models looked very trendy in their sports gear. They strutted on stage with tennis racquets, badminton racquets and basketballs. The classic Michael Jackson number 'Jam' was playing in the background, as the models sashayed in style.

The team then got busy readying for the Western attire round, when Nafisa realized that one of the tarpaulin cloth walls in their changing room had come loose. The girls had not yet finished changing and they started screaming.

Rajat and Raghav heard them shriek and quickly reached the ladies' changing tent. They figured out that one of the poles had fallen down. Raghav lifted the pole and pushed it into the ground, while Rajat pulled the ropes that held the cloth and tied them strongly to the pole. They were about to leave the room when the pole again began to fall again. Raghav quickly caught it and shouted to the girls, 'Get ready quickly. I'll hold the pole till you are done.'

Through the gap between the tent cloth, Nafisa could see Raghav standing tall with his loosely knotted tie. She had never realized how handsome he was. Between wearing her business suit and putting on her make-up, she tried to get a glimpse of Raghav through the gap in the tent. She smiled to herself seeing him stand there like a mannequin holding the pole supporting the tent. She found him cute and chuckled to herself. Time had flown so fast in these four years that she'd hardly got a chance to get to know him better.

In the Western attire round, the girls looked smart in suits and skirts. The boys also looked dashing in tuxedos, tweed jackets and overcoats. Their performance ended with the models waving the Indian national flag and swaying to patriotic music.

Team Mathewson felt that despite the faux pas, they had done a fairly good job.

Diwan Chand College was the last team to perform and they put up a very elaborate show. The models looked professional with well-toned bodies and practiced gait.

Soon, it was time for the results. Tulika Ghosh, a former Miss India, was ready to announce the results.

'I'd like to congratulate all the teams for putting up such a grand show. As I saw you all on stage, I remembered my own modelling days. It was very tough to decide the winner. Without much ado, let me announce the results. Starting with the third prize, the winner is Kelkar College of Engineering, Bombay.'

The team from Kelkar went ballistic as they went up the stage to collect their prize.

'The second prize goes to Venky College, Chennai.'

Without much hullaballoo, the team captain from the college went up to collect the prize.

The Mathewson College camp was quiet. They knew it was all over for them.

On a large screen next to the stage, the fashion show was being replayed. Sujoy noticed their last act being played over and over again. At first, he couldn't understand why but when he looked carefully, he was shocked. One of the national flags a model was swaying was inverted. Instead of saffron, the white stripe was at the top. The Diwan Chand team discovered this and repeatedly played the clip on the large screen to make sure the judges saw it. Sujoy couldn't believe it. They had missed out this important detail and now it would be over for them. Sujoy held his head in his hands and shook it with frustration.

There was total silence in the crowd as Tulika got ready to announce the winner.

'And now for the first prize. No prizes for guessing. It is none other than Diwan Chand College for their mind-blowing performance.'

The home crowd was absolutely over the moon. This was the most popular event and they had once again proven they were the best.

Mathewson College was shocked to hear the results. Sujoy held his head in hands. He knew it was all over for them. He saw all the team members pick up their bags slowly, ready to leave.

Raghav walked up to Sujoy patted him on his back, 'Don't worry, I think we all enjoyed the experience.'

Rajat was disappointed and walked up to Sujoy. He couldn't believe they hadn't won a single prize. He looked at Sujoy and said, 'I think we didn't have the right people on the team. I felt even our theme was too common. There was nothing interesting in it. Look at the way the Diwan Chand guys crafted their performance. It was amazing. The ways they used the props was innovative.'

Sujoy looked at Rajat and asked, 'Do you have the events brochure?'

Rajat replied, 'Hmm. Let me check my bag.'

Sujoy flipped through the brochure and stopped at one of the pages. He got up suddenly.

'Rajat, follow me.'

Sujoy started walking quickly towards the stage with the brochure in his hand. He approached the section where the judges were seated but was blocked by the organizers.

'You can't go there,' growled one of the boys.

Sujoy was in no mood to take no for an answer and elbowed his way straight up to Tulika Ghosh's seat.

'Excuse me, ma'am, do you have a moment?'

Tulika turned around and smiled at Sujoy. She thought he was an eager fan who wanted her autograph.

'Yes, tell me.'

'We are from Mathewson College and our team participated in the fashion show. Here is the brochure with rules for the event that all the teams were supposed to follow. Let me read them out for you.

The allotted time for each team on the ramp is twenty minutes.

No dangerous props such as fire, sharp objects, etc. should be used during the show.

The outfits must not be lewd.

Teams that violate even one of the above rules will be disqualified without any explanation.

Our team followed each of the rules. But one of the teams has violated the rules. Diwan Chand College used fire props in their ethnic round. Even their performance was more than forty-five minutes. More than double the allotted time. How can they be given the first prize if they have violated the rules?' asked Sujoy confidently.

Sujoy's argument made Tulika think.

Tulika turned around to the other judges. They started whispering among each other. One of the professors from Diwan Chand, who was also a judge, listened to Tulika and then gave Sujoy a disgusted look. He knew this boy was up to something.

Tulika then said, 'You are right, the rules have been violated.' She stood up and walked up the stage, as the emcee finished making an announcement.

Tulika took the microphone from him and said, 'Ladies and gentlemen, I have an announcement to make. This may not go down well with the home team, but we need to remember that every game has its rules. It has come to our notice that the home team violated the rule of not using dangerous props. Hence, it will be disqualified. So, the other winners move one position up. The team that was fourth will get the third prize. Can I please ask someone from the Fusion team from Mathewson Technical College to come up and collect the prize?'

Sujoy heaved a sigh of relief and got on the stage to collect the third prize.

'Well done!'

'Thank you, ma'am.'

'You did the right thing. Always fight for your right. Even I've done these things before. But be careful about the flag in the future,' said Tulika and laughed.

Sujoy too laughed with her.

After the event, Sujoy and Rajat were about to get onto their scooter when they saw some of their team members walking back dejected.

Sujoy stopped in front of them.

'Stop sulking, guys. There's some great news. We won the third prize. Diwan Chand violated the rules and were disqualified.'

The other team members were ecstatic hearing this and hugged each other.

Raghav punched his fist in the air with repeated chants of, 'Yes, yes!' He looked at Sujoy with respect and shook his hand.

'Thanks buddy,' said Raghav.

After the celebrations that went on till late in the evening, Raghav went back to his hostel room.

He changed and got into bed to sleep. He had barely laid down for a few minutes when he suddenly woke up. He switched on his table lamp and took out his diary from the drawer. He was reflecting on the event that day and how he'd unknowingly stumbled onto something.

He wrote the date on the top of the page and began writing.

'All decisions in life are made either from the head or the heart. Knowing when to use what is a journey called life.'

THE DIARY

'The only thing that is left to order now is the cheque.,' said Raghav.

The group left the restaurant after tipping Bob generously for playing along with their mood and for looking after them so well. They also giving him a round of applause.

As Shivam was shaking hands before leaving, he heard a beep on his phone. He took out the phone from his pocket.

'Eight messages! Whose are these? Let me check. Holy shit! These are debits from my credit card. Somebody has hacked my card. Somebody has been swiping my card. This is over thousand dollars. Oh my God! I need to call the police,' he said with a pronounced slur in his voice.

Suddenly, Shivam started laugh wildly. 'I forgot that before coming here I had given my card to my wife for shopping. I told her that I would be gone only for two hours. I guess I've got a fitting punishment for this late-night fun.'

The others couldn't control themselves and burst out laughing. Shivam hastily waved goodbye to everyone and rushed out.

The others also left soon after. Raghav stopped by at the Alamo cube again. This time it was still, shimmering in the light of the streetlights. Only a young couple was sitting at the base of the sculpture. At the subway, Raghav's train arrived and he found an empty seat. He looked around the carriage. An old man was sitting all by himself. A Chinese couple seemed to be on their way back home, possibly after closing their shop for the day. A wobbling drunk man walked passed by. A group of girls, probably tourists from a European country, sat giggling at the far end of the carriage.

It was late and he was feeling sleepy. He closed his eyes and started to recall the conversations of the evening when his mind wandered to the subject of the meeting request that Nafisa had sent. 'LOL evening.' 'LOL. Huh. Ha ha,' Raghav muttered to himself, his eyes shut. 'LOL. LOL. Ha ha! Lessons on Life.'

He opened his eyes to see people staring at him. He just smiled.

When Raghav got home, he began to reminiscence about college days. How time had flown! Life today was so different from those days.

He smiled to himself when he recalled the Fashion Show they had put up. It was such a crazy idea but so much fun. Thanks to Sujoy he was able to do this spur-of-the-moment act that he normally wouldn't have even dreamt of. He wondered where he was now.

Those days, while practising for the event, he also got to know Nafisa better. They'd spent some nice times together. He remembered that one evening after practice he'd dropped her off at the girl's hostel. She wouldn't stop talking about her life in Pune. In that short walk he'd come to know practically everything about her. He'd got to know about her joint family, her cousins, her parents, where she liked eating, her favourite movie stars, her most hated movie stars. Which cousin was the naughtiest, which cousin followed which passion. Why she chose engineering. What were her dreams. Though he'd only listened, he'd wished the walk to the hostel was longer.

He also recalled the insane leg pulling that he'd undergone in the hostel when he'd got back.

She hadn't changed much or at least that's what he could make out from last evening. She was still her vivacious bubbly self.

His mind went back to his diary. Back in the days he used to be so obsessed about writing every day. Come hell or high water he would never miss a chance to scribble notes in his diary. He recalled the diaries he would bring back home after each semester end and his mother would want to throw them away. How he would argue with her and somehow convince her to find a place for them.

As life moved on, that habit of writing also moved on. Today it was a distant memory.

He recalled the line he'd written after the Fashion Show.

All decisions in life are made either from the head or the heart. Knowing when to use what is a journey called life.

It was simple, yet profound. He wished he could get the diary where he wrote these lines. He wondered where would that diary be.

Did he throw it somewhere? Was it packed somewhere in an old trunk? Was it in his father's garage in their new house in Indore's Saket Nagar?

He was yearning to get hold of his old diary. He felt like a child who had suddenly remembered a favourite toy and now wanted it badly.

Raghav felt the diary was like a key. A key that would open something inside him.

KURT JANSON

A couple of days later, Raghav called up Max from the media team at VisionTek.

'Max, I need your help. Can I get the address of the boy whose hand was injured because of the Glove?'

'Why? What happened?'

'I need to speak to him'

'Let me try, Raghav. The newspaper reporter who broke the news should have it.'

A few days later, Max sent an email to Raghav with the details of the boy.

Raghav thought of calling the boy, but he couldn't muster the courage. He just did not know what to expect. Finally, after two days of mulling over, Raghav picked up the phone.

'Hi, am I speaking to Kurt Janson?'

'Yes, this is Kurt.'

Raghav was a little taken back by the softness of the voice. On the phone Kurt seemed a lot younger than his images in the news.

'This is Raghav from VisionTek.'

'VisionTek. You, you fuckers! What do you want now?!'

Clearly, the anger was pent-up in the young boy and Raghav's call had triggered its release.

'Kurt, I'm sorry about what happened to you. This is really unfortunate.'

'You are sorry? Great! But then what happens to the three months I lost in school? My hand is not the same as before. I don't think I will ever play baseball again.'

'Kurt, I would like to meet you.'

Just then, Raghav would hear an older voice get involved in the conversation. Raghav could make out the father and son were having a chat.

'Why do you want to meet us?'

The senior Janson's voice conveyed pure unadulterated anger.

'Sir, I'm Raghav. I was the head of product management at VisionTek. I'm deeply saddened by what has happened to your son and would like to apologize to him in person.'

Janson Senior was aware of the machinations of the corporate world and agreed to Raghav's request to see the 'new trick' they had up their sleeve.

The next Sunday afternoon, Raghav reached the Janson residence in Springfield, New Jersey. He parked his car on the road and walked up to the porch. On the way he saw a child's bicycle and a half-chewed Frisbee lying on the ground. By now, he'd gone through so many possible scenarios in his head, about what could happen, that he was feeling a lot more confident about facing the family.

Kurt's younger brother answered the door.

Raghav sat in their living room, waiting for the rest of the family. He was nervous.

After a while, the entire Janson family walked in. The senior Mr Janson started the conversation.

'You are here to convince me to not sue your company. Right?'

'No, Mr. Janson. There's a misunderstanding.'

'I hope you understand we've filed a personal injury lawsuit against your company. So, what action you take today can have a bearing on the case.'

Raghav was paying attention to Mr Janson, but at same time he was distracted by Kurt's palm that had a dark burn patch in the centre.

'Mr Janson, I'm no longer employed with VisionTek. I was fired right after the incident. Perhaps you missed the news.'

Raghav got up and took out a cheque from his jacket. Senior Mr Janson's gaze became intent.

'Mr Janson, I know this may not make you feel better, but this will help lift some weight off my chest. Please accept this.'

Mrs Jansen and Kurt glanced at each other.

Mr Jansen got up and took the cheque from Raghav. He was not interested in the cheque but wanted to know whose account it was.

The name of the account holder was that of Raghav Diwan. For the first time in the conversation, Mr Jansen's eyes relaxed.

That was enough for Raghav. He didn't want to stand there any longer. Without saying a word, he walked out.

Raghav got into the car and dialled his travel agent from the office and asked him to book flights for India.

Raghav called Tarana and told her that he would be coming to Indore soon.

BHIMBETKA

Raghav's flight landed at Indore's Devi Ahilya Bai Holkar airport. He always liked the first few hours when he arrived in India. That's the time when he felt a deep sense of optimism about India's future. To Raghav, India was like an elephant on skates. Though it was colossal, there was now a spring in its step.

He caught a taxi and headed home to Saket Nagar. On the way, he asked the driver to stop by the famous Sarafa Bazaar. He had never done that on any previous trip but today was different. He wanted to let in the memories of his childhood flood his mind. He didn't want the driver to spend too much time there. All he wanted was a glimpse. It was evening and the streets were teeming with people, mostly families wanting to enjoy good street food.

Sarafa Bazaar was a busy jewellery bazaar during the day and street food court at night. When Raghav was young, during festivals, his mother would drag the family out for jewellery shopping. She either bought something new or exchanged some of her old stuff. It was only later that he found that most of those transactions were actually meant for his future wife. Little did his mother know that though her daughter-in-law took the jewellery to the US, she would hardly ever wear any of it.

It had been six years since he had lost his mother. But somehow, he missed her more when he was in India. Even his father seemed to miss her more when they came home.

***

Raghav's father, Tarana and the kids were elated to see him. The boys were eager to see what toys their father had brought them. They kept asking him about the neighbour's dog and if they would get to walk him when they got back.

Raghav spent the next week overcoming his jet lag and answering questions every few hours on what would he like for his meals.

'Papa, I heard from Tarana that your consulting is going well,' said Raghav.

'Early days, *beta.* You know how demanding consulting can be,' said his father.

***

One afternoon, when everyone was asleep, Raghav decided to go to the garage.

His father's garage was very different from his neat and organized garage back home in the US. There were old boxes piled haphazardly on top of each other. One corner was occupied by an old, rusty washing machine and his father's broken harmonium. Another corner had a huge pile of old newspapers. Raghav was tempted to start cleaning the garage but he decided to focus on the task at hand.

Raghav opened a trunk and pulled out plastic bags full of books. He did the same for a few more trunks. With bundles of books around him, he sat down on the floor to look for his diary. He went through each pile carefully.

He found old semester project reports, autograph books, an expired university swimming pool ID card, old photographs and a few half-used diaries. He picked up the bundle of diaries and sat down on the floor. Most of the diaries contained class notes; only a few were his daily diary. He opened one of his daily dairies. The writing seemed familiar but at the same time strange. Time had taken a toll on his handwriting, too. The handwriting in his diary was neat and tidy whereas today he only scribbled 'to do' lists on any sheet he could get hold of.

He quickly scanned through the diary. But no luck with those lines he was looking for. He picked up the next diary. The result was the same. He went through three more diaries and still nothing. He started from the first diary again, this time reading through it carefully. He even tried to correlate the dates but the search was a failure.

His neck began to hurt. He stretched his legs and started wondering where his diary could be. The fatigue and the heat in the garage made him drowsy. He pulled out an old newspaper lying around, rolled it, put it under his head, and closed his eyes.

It must have been about an hour when he heard a few voices in the background

'Papa, papa,' shouted his boys, looking inside the half-opened garage.

Their shouting woke up Raghav. He woke up slowly, feeling well rested. The boys looked at their father with a surprised expression wondering what their father was doing on the floor.

The lines he wrote suddenly came back to him. 'All decisions in life are made from the head or the heart. Knowing when to use what is a journey called life.' Today the absoluteness of these lines made them seem like a formula created by a scholar. A formula that was correct but also reflected the naivety of the scholar's youth. Over time, these lines seemed to have acquired a different meaning. Giving human beings a head and a heart seemed to be the universe's way of complicating their lives. Lives in which they can ponder whether they were right or wrong in the application of the formula but have few opportunities to change the outcome.

That evening, Raghav sat down with his father for evening tea.

'Papa, I was thinking about your idea.'

'Which idea?' asked his father, picking up a biscuit.

'The one about educating people about India's history?'

'Yes, what about it? You were saying it was not worth it.'

'I gave it a second thought. Maybe if we build a game around the concept, kids will find it interesting,' said Raghav with a hint of an apology.

'Hmm… I thought it was a good idea. Let's plan sometime next week to discuss it in detail.'

'Papa, in the corporate world we always say the deadline was yesterday. Let's start work from today,' replied Raghav.

'Okay, that's even better,' said his father, with a laugh.

For the next few weeks, Raghav was busy contacting people in his network with a gaming background. Once he got some direction, he started work on the design. He had no prior experience in designing a game and relied mostly on his intuition.

He turned the guest bedroom into his project office. The wall was now covered by a couple of whiteboards. He also got a table setup for his laptop and printer.

In some time, he was able to create the design of the game. He was quite happy with the screen layouts but realized he needed to put some historical context into the design. He wondered which monument or archaeological site he should choose.

***

One morning, Raghav woke up to see Tarana working on her laptop.

'So early? What happened?'

'After coming here, I have been setting up accounts for papa to pay the utility bills. Today I realized that I hadn't paid the electricity and water bills. I want to finish it before the boys wake up.'

'That's good. Do you want some coffee? I'm making some for myself.'

'Sure, I don't mind.'

Raghav was busy in the kitchen, when suddenly his younger son woke up and started shouting.

'Tarana, see what he wants. I'll do the billing. What's the user ID and the password?'

'I was trying to reset the password. Please check my mail box. You'll find the new password.'

'Okay.'

Raghav sat down with his cup of coffee and opened Tarana's laptop. He clicked on her Gmail account and saw the email from the electricity department with the new password. He was about to enter the new password when a familiar name in Tarana's email inbox caught his attention.

Harpreet.

What were Harpreet's mail doing here? He looked around to make sure Tarana wasn't looking.

He opened Harpreet's last email.

Hi Tarana,

Hope Raghav is back and things are settling down now. 'Drop me a line when you get the time.'

Raghav saw more mails from Harpreet.

As he scrolled down further, he saw another familiar name. Nafisa. Raghav tried hard to control his mind from manufacturing theories.

Raghav opened the mail with the subject 'Thanks' and scrolled to the first mail in the thread.

Dear Nafisa and Harpreet,

Thank you so much for helping out. If you two had not planned the get-together, I don't know what would have happened to Raghav. I was so scared. Harpreet, thank you for giving the idea to get Nafisa to contact Raghav.

Nafisa, I can't thank you enough for what do you did.

Love,
Tarana

Raghav then read Nafisa's reply.

Dear Tarana,

Please! Don't even mention it. I'm not even sure it was because of the get-to-

gether, but I'm happy you think it helped. Sometimes, I think life teaches us lessons that get buried under the dust of time. Once in a while, it's good to blow that dust away and see what we can find.

When are you back? We definitely need to catch up over coffee.

Cheers!
Nafisa.

Raghav stopped for a moment trying to absorb what he had read. He sipped his coffee and opened his own email account to distract himself. Since he hadn't opened his emails in a while there were several hundred unread emails.

He was glancing through them leisurely when his eyes were drawn to an email from a VisionTek ID. The subject read- 'Urgent | Response to Legal notice.' Raghav read through it quickly. VisionTek was suing him for negligence and had sent a legal notice to his house. They had probably found that he was in India and had followed it up with an email.

Raghav didn't bother much about the email and shut down his laptop. He was so preoccupied with the game that he didn't want to waste time thinking about the impending legal implications . He was thinking about what historical background to give the game when it occurred to him that the Bhimbetka Rock Shelters were close by to be explored for the concept of the game.

His father's trusted driver Ramakant was summoned to organize a Toyota Innova for the trip to Bhimbetka. When Raghav told the boys about the five-hour drive their eyes immediately lit up.

They were off early morning to explore the rock shelters exhibiting the beginning of the Indian stone age. Tarana was relieved to see them all together again. After a couple of hours they stopped at a roadside eatery to grab a bite and stretch their legs. They settled down on a rickety table and ordered a light breakfast.

The waiter brought Raghav his omelette. Raghav was about to eat it but was suddenly hit by a thought.

'I'm going to the car, will be back in a minute', said Raghav and rushed to the Innova.

He pulled out an old diary from his college days that he'd thrown into his bag. He flipped through the pages desperately looking for an empty page. He found it had entries that he had made during his last semester in 1998. He found a new page, put today's date and wrote.

'The Universe tries to reveal its plan for you. If you get what it is, don't mess with it.'

Raghav then returned to Tarana and the boys to finish his breakfast. Soon they were off on their way. Raghav took a snooze for some time but woke up suddenly to ask Tarana a question that was bothering him for a while. 'What do you think I should name the game?'

Tarana paused for a moment from the article she was reading on her iPad and said, 'How about Rewind and Play?'

DISCLAIMER

The author bears no responsibility, if as a result of reading this book, the reader encounters mishappenings such as but not limited to – wrecking his/her married life after connecting with an old flame; losing a dear friend for bringing up a forgotten incident; giving up a job for starting something new. ☺

Dear Reader,

I am indebted to you for picking up this book and becoming a part of my world. Please connect with me on teegeesbooks (twitter) & Facebook. I would love to know the emotions, thoughts and memories the book evoked after you read it. Also, eager to read interesting anecdotes from your college days.

Sincerely,
Tarun Gautam

ABOUT THE AUTHOR

Tarun Gautam is an IIM Lucknow alumnus working for a leading technology firm as a Regional Sales Manager in international markets. In his eighteen years of experience, he has worked in Europe and Africa and travelled to twenty countries across several continents.

He has also played a key role in the early stages of two management consulting start-ups.

Tarun takes a keen interest in social initiatives and environment related issues. He was involved in the 'Let's Do it Delhi' campaign to create awareness about cleanliness in the city. He recently shared a proposal with the Delhi government to implement Work-from-Home across companies to reduce vehicular pollution and traffic in the city.

He enjoys playing golf, doing yoga and spending time with his daughter.

Website: www.tarungautam.com

Facebook: facebook.com/TarunGautamAuthor

Twitter: @teegeesbooks

Write to Tarun at: teegee@tarungautam.com